The Adventures of Molly Whuppie

and Other Appalachian Folktales

ANNE SHELBY

Illustrations by Paula McArdle

THE UNIVERSITY OF NORTH CAROLINA PRESS

CHAPEL HILL

THE ADVENTURES OF

Molly Whuppie

and Other Appalachian Folktales

TO GABRIELLE

Clever, Strong, and Brave

© 2007 Anne Shelby
Illustrations © 2007 Paula McArdle / illustrationOnLine.com
All rights reserved
Manufactured in United States of America
Set in Fresco Sans   Designed by Richard Hendel
The paper in this book meets the guidelines for permanence and durability of the Committee on
Production Guidelines for Book Longevity of the Council on Library Resources.

"Jack and the Christmas Beans" previously appeared, in slightly different form, in *A Kentucky
Christmas*, edited by George Ella Lyon (Lexington: University Press of Kentucky, 2003).

Library of Congress Cataloging-in-Publication Data
Shelby, Anne.
The adventures of Molly Whuppie and other Appalachian folktales /
Anne Shelby ; illustrations by Paula McArdle.
p. cm.
Contents: The adventures of Molly Whuppie—Molly the giant slayer—Tater toe—
Molly and Blunderbore —Molly Fiddler—Runaway cornbread—Molly and the ogre who would
not pick up—Pig tale—Molly and the unwanted boyfriends—Grind mill grind—Jack and the
Christmas beans—Molly and Jack—Molly, Jack, and the sillies—Just past dreaming rock.
Includes bibliographical references.
ISBN 978-0-8078-3163-2 (cloth : alk. paper)
[1. Folklore—Appalachian region.] I. McArdle, Paula, ill. II. Title.
PZ8.1.S5388Ad 2007
398.20974'03274—dc22
2007013789

11 10 09 08 07   5 4 3 2 1

: The Stories :

:The Adventures of Molly Whuppie:

I reckon you've heard about Jack, the boy that climbed a beanstalk and outsharped a giant and all.

I bet you know about Cinderella, too. And the three bears and the three little pigs and the three billy goats gruff. But did you ever hear of a girl named Molly Whuppie?

Molly Whuppie lived way back. Way back in time. Way back in the mountains, too. W-a-a-a-a-a-a-y back. With her mommy and her daddy and her sisters Poll and Betts. Their right names were Polly and Betsy, but to save time everybody just called them Poll and Betts.

Well, one brave day Poll and Betts got it in their heads to go off and have adventures. Their daddy was away from home working at the time, so he had no say in the matter. Their mommy said, well, she reckoned they could go, and she started in baking journey cakes. Journey cakes are what people in folktales eat whenever they go on a trip. They're like a biscuit but with a little pinch of magic added in. And not so much baking powder.

Well, the mommy was just putting the journey cakes in the oven when into the kitchen marched Molly Whuppie, with her bonnet tied around her neck and her tricks packed in a poke. "I aim to go, too," she announced.

"Oh no you ain't!" declared Poll and Betts, both at the very same time.

"You'd be a pretty thing a-sailing down the road," smirked Betts.

"And you no bigger than a smidgen," put in Poll. Molly was the least one, and Poll and Betts, being older, had got to thinking they were grown women, when really they were just big gangly girls. Anyway, they made it plain they'd have no little sister tagalong.

Molly Whuppie could pitch a fit when she wanted to. She hollered and cried and stomped her foot and held her breath and took on the worst ever was till finally her mother, just to get a minute's peace, said, "Molly Sally Whuppie, you hush that right now! I'll let you go, but first you'll have to fetch a bucketful of water from the creek so I can make your journey cakes." So Molly took the bucket, and off she went to the creek.

"Don't let her go with us, Mommy!" Poll and Betts whined in unison.

"She'll ruin the whole trip," fussed Poll.

"If she goes I ain't a-going," fumed Betts.

"Hush. She ain't a-going," Mommy whispered. "That bucket's full of holes. She can't carry water in that. You two go on now before she gets back." So Poll and Betts slipped off and left.

Molly, in the meantime, was busy trying to fill a holey bucket up with water. Well, naturally every time she went to fill it up, it spewed right back out. She did that six or seven times and was about to try it again when she heard the flutter of bird wings and saw a little bird light on a tree limb overhead. And the little bird sang a little song:

Daub it with moss and stick it with clay
Then you can carry your water away.

Molly didn't understand all the words at first, not being used to bird-talk. Then she closed her eyes and listened hard:

Daub it with moss and stick it with clay
Then you can carry your water away.

Then Molly Whuppie didn't do a thing in this world but take that bucket, daub it with moss, stick it with clay, fill it with water, and carry it away, up the hill and back to the house and straight to her mother's kitchen.

Well, her mommy was surprised to see that bucket full of water, you may be sure of that. But she'd always told the girls, "Girls," she told them, "you have got to do what you say you'll do." So she had to make Molly some journey cakes and let her go on the trip, for that is what she said she'd do if Molly fetched the water.

Molly took her journey cakes and ran down the road as hard as she could go, waving her arms and hollering for Poll and Betts to wait up. They tried to get away from her, but Molly could run so much faster than they could, she caught up with them in no time.

Then they spied her journey cakes. They had already eaten all theirs about five minutes after they left the house. "Come here, little Molly," they said, sweet enough to draw flies, "and give us a bite of your journey cakes." Molly divided the cakes with her sisters, and they proceeded on down the road.

Went along, went along, and after while the sun eased down behind the hills and it commenced to get dark. The girls started trying to scope out a place to stay all night. But there was not a house to be found, not a barn, not a shed, not even a cave to crawl in. Walked on, walked on, the night turning colder and blacker by the minute, till finally they spied a light a-burning way off yonder in the woods. And they started toward that light.

They came to a dark lonesome place hid back deep in the woods. Grapevines hung like nooses from the trees. As the girls walked toward the house, briars grabbed at their dress-tails and scratched their hands and ankles.

Were they scared? Well, naturally. But by that time they were so tired and so hungry, they didn't much care what happened, so long as they got to sit down for it and had something nice to eat first.

Molly stood at the gate and hollered. In a dark window a strange face appeared. Then the door opened and out stepped a big high tall giant woman. "Who are you and what do you want?" she demanded.

"We're just three little girls out lost on the road," Betts answered, as humbly as she could manage.

"We're wore out and close to starvation," Poll added, in her most pitiful voice. This made Poll and Betts feel so sorry for themselves they both busted out a-crying.

"Well, come on in then," the big high tall giant woman told them. But you could tell by the way she said it she was not much in the mood for company.

She'd already eat her supper, but she pulled the leftovers out of the warming closet and gave them to the girls to eat.

Then she said to Poll and Betts, "You two can sleep up in the loft with my two girls. They're already up there with their white nightcaps on." Then she went in the other room and came back with two more nightcaps, only these were red, red as blood, and she handed them to Poll and Betts.

"Put these on," she said. "Hit gets chilly in the loft of a night." So Poll and Betts put the red nightcaps on and climbed up in the loft and went to sleep beside the giant's girls.

The big high tall giant woman told Molly to sleep in the bed with her. "And be my little grandbaby," she said.

"All right, Granny," Molly answered, and she crawled in the bed and fell asleep, just like that.

But away up in the night, Molly Whuppie woke up. And she heard the big high tall giant woman saying rhymes in her sleep:

Fee fie fo fum
Look out girlies here I come.
Fee fie fo—when you're fast asleep
Up into the loft I'll creep.
Knock the red nightcaps in the head
Lock 'em in the cellar and bake 'em into bread.

When the giant woman finished her poem, she rolled over and went to snoring.

Real quiet Molly Whuppie slipped out of the bed and sneaked up in the loft. Real quiet she pulled all the nightcaps off and switched them around, the red caps to the giant's girls' heads, the white nightcaps to Poll and Betts. Real quiet she stepped back down the ladder and crawled back in the bed.

After while Molly heard an awful commotion, which was, of course, the giant woman hitting her own girls over the head with a plank and dragging them down from the loft and locking them in the cellar. Oh, they squealed and squalled and took on a sight, but the giant woman didn't pay a bit of attention to that. She was used to that. After she got them locked up, she got back in the bed and went to snoring again.

Molly Whuppie laid there awake till daylight. Then she went and woke up Poll and Betts. "We've got to get out of here," she said.

As they ran through the yard, Molly broke off a little briar and handed it to Poll. "Put that down in your pocket, Poll," she told her. As they passed by the henhouse, she picked up a chicken egg. "Put that down in your pocket, Betts," she said. Down in her own pocket, Molly Whuppie slipped a little flat rock.

Well, they moved as rapid as they could, but after while they heard the giant coming up behind them. They had a good head start on her, but the giant woman was wearing her seven-mile-step boots, so every time she took a step she went seven miles. So here she was coming up on them.

Molly told Poll, said, "Poll, throw that briar back over your shoulder." Poll threw it back, and a big thick jungle of briars sprung up between them and the giant. She had to fight her way through that, which took her a good while. But she got out of it finally and here she came again.

Molly hollered at Betts, "Betts, throw that egg back over your shoulder." Betts threw it back, and a big lake of egg yolks flowed all over the countryside. The giant had to swim the egg yolk lake, which slowed her down a right smart. But after while here she came again.

Molly reached down in her pocket and threw back that little flat rock. And in less time than it takes to tell it, big mountain ranges reared up out of the ground, and while the giant was climbing them, the girls pulled out ahead.

But it wasn't long till here she came again, and the girls had run out of anything to throw back. The giant marched right up to them in her seven-mile-steppers. And she was mad, you could tell.

"I am bad put out with you, Molly Whuppie," she said. "I wanted you to be my little grandbaby, and here you've caused me to have to climb up and down big mountain ranges, swim in egg yolks, get caught in briar patches, and knock my own girls in the head with a plank."

Then she pulled a sack out of her pocket and said to Poll, "You jump in my puddin-tuddin bag!" Poll got scared and fell right in.

Then the giant looked at Betts. "You jump in my puddin-tuddin bag!" Betts got scared, too, and dived in the bag head foremost.

Then the giant turned to Molly Whuppie and said, "Now, little missy, you jump in my puddin-tuddin bag!"

Before you could say "Jack Robinson," Molly Whuppie had grabbed that sack and dumped her sisters out on the ground. "No, ma'am!" she hollered at that giant. "YOU jump in MY puddin-tuddin bag!" And the bag sucked the giant down in there.

The girls tied her up good and tight and left her there, kicking and cussing to beat the band. So that took care of the big high tall giant woman, but then the girls had to figure out what to do next.

Poll and Betts said they'd had about all the adventure they could stand for a while, thank you very much, and were all for going straight home and taking a good long nap.

"Fiddlesticks!" said Molly Whuppie. "Just when the trip was getting interesting!" For Molly Whuppie had found that she liked fooling with giants and felt that she had a certain talent for it.

Finally the sisters came to an agreement. They'd go back home that day and come back and have some more adventures later on. And Poll and Betts swore and declared that the next time they took a notion to go out in the big world, they definitely absolutely positively and without a doubt wanted Little Sister to go, too. They could not possibly do without her, they said, and would she promise right then and there that she'd go.

Molly grinned. "Well, I might go," she said, "if you beg me."

: Molly the Giant Slayer :

At the time this next adventure took place, the Whuppies were all living up at the head of Hoot Owl Holler.

And they were well satisfied up there. They liked seeing the sun of a morning, popping up big and sudden behind the east hill. They liked watching it of an evening, too, putting on a big show of pink and orange, slipping down behind the west ridge.

They liked the smells of sassafras and honeysuckle, the sound of creek water dancing over rocks, and the songs the wind played in the treetops on the mountain. They liked having their friends and their kinfolks close around them.

But they had their troubles, too, like anybody else. They were not rich people, the Whuppies were not. To tell you the truth, they didn't have much of anything at all, but just one another and some very nice scenery.

Not that they were afraid of work. They were not. Many a day they worked daylight to dark, just as hard as they could go. Hoeing, hewing, hauling, planting, plowing, picking and pickling, grubbing newgrounds, cutting timber, drawing water, and digging coal. But their little old farm was steep as a mule's face, and no matter how hard they worked, they could not make a go.

So the Whuppie family decided that, bad as they hated to, they'd have to leave Hoot Owl Holler and see if they couldn't do better somewhere else. They loaded their few belongings on the wagon, put on their hats, put out the fire, whistled for the dog, and lit out.

Well, they traveled all that day and on into the evening till it got too dark to see. So they decided they'd pull over for the night, sleep in the wagon, and get a good early start the next morning.

Then they got to thinking, maybe somebody ought to stay up all night and keep a lookout. They didn't know that country, didn't know what might be around in there. Might be bears. Might be robbers. Might be giants. They didn't know. Somebody had to sit up. But who?

"Not me," volunteered Poppy Whuppie. "I'm wore out from driving this mule and wagon."

Molly the Giant Slayer : : : 9

"My nerves is shot," Mommy Whuppie declared, and she swore she could not sit up all night if they paid her a million dollars.

Betts said if she didn't get her sleep, she'd drag around and feel bad the whole next day.

"Don't look at me!" said Poll. "I'd be scared to death."

But Molly Whuppie did not know the meaning of afraid. "Shoot, I'll do it," she said. "I ain't a bit sleepy." So they all went to bed and left Molly sitting up.

Molly picked up a handful of little flat rocks and put them in her pocket. Then she climbed to the top of a tall pine tree, where she could keep a good lookout. Stayed up there all night, Molly did, and didn't hear a thing but toad frogs, whippoorwills, and one old screech owl.

Along about daylight, Molly got so sleepy it was all she could do to keep from falling out of her tree. And then all of a sudden she heard the biggest racket ever was. Looked over there and what did she see? Two giants building a cook-fire. They'd been out all night stealing hogs, which they were now about to cook for breakfast.

Oh, they were mean-looking, both of them, and big, even for giants. For their spoons they used shovels, and pitchforks for their forks.

Well, this one giant, he got him a big hunk of hog meat on his fork and was just about to put it in his mouth when Molly Whuppie cut loose with a rock. That rock hit that meat, knocked it clean off the giant's fork, and sent it a-flying. Which caused the giant to job his own chin with a pitchfork and holler he was killed. "I'm kilt!" he hollered.

So the very next thing he did was start looking around for somebody to blame it on. He looked up and saw his brother over there, so he blamed it on him. "What did you go and do that for?" he asked him. "I'll come over there and smack the fire out of you!"

Well, his brother took offense at that, on the grounds that he did not like being accused of jobbing people in the chin with pitchforks when he had not done a thing in this world but just sit there and try to eat meat. "I never tipped you," he said, "and you better not say I did! I'll whup your hind end all over this hillside!"

That's one thing about a giant. They cannot settle any kind of a dispute in a reasonable manner. Any little disagreement comes up, they get in a splutterment over it. Splutterment escalates to upscuddle, and next thing you know the fur's a-flying.

They quarreled and fussed around a while, and then the second giant went to take him a bite of hog meat. He raised that big fork up to his mouth, and about that time Molly cut loose with another rock. Clipped the meat clean off that giant's fork and caused him to job his chin and holler out he was killed, too. "I'm kilt!" he hollered.

Then he looked his brother in the eye and said, "You've caused me to gouge a hole in my purdy chin, and I aim to skin you alive!"

Well, that made the other one so mad he hauled off and hit that one over the head with the flat of a shovel and raised a big pump knot on his head. They lit in to fighting. And they fought and they fit and they fought and they fit and they fought and they fit some more. Knocking down big trees, rocks a-rolling downhill, giant hair and giant teeth a-flying ever which away.

Well, that tickled Molly Whuppie so good, she laughed right out loud. She started laughing, got her tickle box turned over, and could not quit. The longer she laughed, the louder she laughed, and the louder she laughed, the longer she laughed, till finally the giants heard her.

"Lay off whompin' and listen a minute," one giant said to the other. "I believe I hear somebody laughin'." That's one more thing about a giant. They cannot stand to be laughed at. That makes them madder than anything. So they quit fighting and went to investigate. And they found a girl up a tree.

"Are you laughin' at us?" they asked her.

"I reckon I am," Molly said, laughing so hard the tears streamed down her face.

"Are you the one caused us to lose our meat and job our chins with forks and fight?"

"I reckon I am," Molly said, laughing so hard her sides hurt.

"Well, we aim to kill you," said the giants. Molly quit laughing.

That's another thing about a giant. First little thing that goes wrong, they're talking about killing somebody.

"Now let's stop and think a minute," Molly said. "You could go ahead and kill me right now . . . " So they started to kill her.

"Or," she added, quick as she could, "maybe I could help you boys some way or another. You're so big, there must be some things that's unhandy for you to do."

The giants thought about that. They were not much used to thinking and not much good at it.

Finally they said, yes, there was one thing. The Queen lived close by, and they'd had it in mind for a while, they said, to get in there and kill the Queen and take over the kingdom. Run things the way they wanted them run. But they never could figure out just how to do it. So they wanted Molly Whuppie to sneak in the castle, kill the Queen, let them in the door, and they'd take it from there.

So that was their plan. Molly didn't think much of it, but it was either that or get killed, so Molly told them she'd go along with it, and they all three went on over to the castle and Molly climbed the wall and got in. She'd used up all her rocks, so she started looking around for something to help her, and she spied a big iron sword a-hanging on the wall. She tried to lift it, but it was way too heavy.

Then she saw a cup a-hanging there, too, with a sign that said DRINK THIS FIRST. Molly drank from the cup, and then when she went to lift the sword again, it was light as a cornstalk, and she could work it around easy.

Molly went to the door where the giants were waiting outside, hollering, "Let us in! What's the holdup? We want in right now!" and all such as that. That's a giant for you. No patience.

"All right, I'll open the door," Molly hollered out to them. "One of you stick your head through, and I'll help you the rest of the way in."

The first giant stuck his big head in the door, and that was as far as he could get. He got stuck and couldn't go this way and couldn't go that. Molly raised that sword, brought it down, and whacked that giant's head off for him.

The second giant couldn't see what was going on, and he started hollering, "I want in, too! That ain't fair! Let me in right now!" and so on. Typical giant—just "me me me."

"All right, you can come in," Molly told him. "But you'll have to push on your brother. He's stuck."

The giant pushed on his brother's hind end till he got him all the way in. Then he stuck his big head in the door, and Molly whacked it off, too.

Then Molly went in there where the Queen was in the bed asleep and woke her up, as gentle as she could. "I'm sorry to bother you this morning, Queen," she said. "But I've got two dead giants out here, and I just wondered what you wanted me to do with them."

"Molly Sally Whuppie," said the Queen. "Do you mean to stand there and tell me that you have killed two big giants already this morning, and me laying here in the bed not knowing a thing about it?"

"Yes, ma'am," Molly said.

"Well, bless your heart," said the Queen. "I've been trying to get rid of them giants for years and years and couldn't. They've stole ever hog in the kingdom. I've had big armies of men in here, and they couldn't do a thing about it. And here you've got rid of them right by yourself."

Then the Queen asked Molly if she would come and work for her and be in charge of Giant Control and Other Giant-Related Matters. She said Molly could live right there in the castle, draw a big salary, and have anything in the world she wanted to eat.

Well, that sounded all right, Molly said, but what about her mommy and her daddy and her sisters Poll and Betts, asleep down in the wagon? Could they come and live, too?

"They shore can," said the Queen. "Go get 'em right now and bring 'em up here."

So Molly went and woke them up and told them all what had happened. After discussing the situation and listing the pros and cons, the Whuppies pulled their wagon up to the front door of the castle.

They lived there with the Queen a long time, the Whuppies did. Molly got the giants under control, and once again the people of the kingdom could keep hogs.

The Queen was quite fond of the Whuppies and treated them the best ever was. They had big piles of money, foreign foods and fancy clothes, gold this and silver that. They had big parties and entertainments going on all the time at the castle, high and mighty folks dropping in day and night, and everything done real proper and just so.

The Whuppies stood it as long as they could. Then one morning before daylight they left the Queen a note, slipped out the back to their little old wagon, and headed home to Hoot Owl Holler.

: Tater Toe :

One time there was a little old woman who lived by herself in a little old house in the shadow of a big old mountain. Out back behind her house the little old woman had a little old garden where she grew peas and parsley, beans and beets, turnips and tomatoes, corn, cucumbers, cauliflower, and cabbage. And potatoes. She grew potatoes out there.

One day the little old woman decided she wanted a mess of peas and potatoes for supper. So she got her hoe and her basket and headed out to the pea and potato patch.

She picked her peas and was in the process of digging her potatoes when she spied this one potato that looked like a toe. It did! It looked for all the world just like a big toe. "Tater toe," she called it.

Now the old woman had been living out there by herself a long time and didn't have much company and didn't go to town much and didn't keep up with the news. So she thought that tater toe was the most exciting thing she had seen or heard tell of since the day the hog broke out of the pen and busted up Sunday school.

The old woman took the tater toe to the house and set it on the kitchen table where she could look at it while she cooked supper. She fixed her a good mess of peas and potatoes, and after she finished supper and washed the dishes, she sat down to look at her tater toe till time to go to bed.

Then she put the tater toe in a canning jar and screwed the lid on good and tight so a mouse wouldn't bother it. She set the jar back down on the kitchen table, bolted the door, blew out the lamp, climbed upstairs to bed, and fell sound asleep as soon as her head hit the pillow, dead to the world.

But sometime up in the night the old woman jerked wide awake. She thought she heard something downstairs, a low growl of a voice whisper, "I WANT MY BIG TOE."

The old woman listened hard for a long minute, but she did not hear another thing. "I must have been dreaming," she told herself, and she rolled over and went back to sleep.

But not too long after that the old woman woke up again. This time she thought she heard something coming up the stairs and a low growl, a little louder this time: "I WANT MY BIG TOE!"

The old woman stayed still as a stone, listening as hard as she could listen, but all she heard was a dog barking somewhere off in the distance and the wind whining around the corners of the house. "Another bad dream," she said to herself, and she pulled the covers up high around her neck and went back to sleep.

The old woman dreamed she was falling off a high cliff, and when she hit the bottom she woke up. That's when she thought she heard the door to her room creak open and a loud growl of a voice demanding, "I WANT MY BIG TOE!!"

The little old woman sat straight up in the bed, peering into the darkness. She saw nothing unusual but the door to her room standing open, and the wind could have been the cause of that. "Bad dream again," she said to herself. But this time it wasn't so easy to get back to sleep.

No matter how she laid in the bed, she could not rest. She tossed and turned. She turned and tossed. She froze one minute and burned up the next. She kicked and yanked and jerked on the covers till she had them upside down, inside out, and wadded up in big knots under the bed. She worried and fretted and imagined till after a while she couldn't tell anymore whether she was awake or asleep.

The next time the little old woman opened her eyes, there was something sitting at the foot of her bed. It was big and hairy and scary and awful, and it howled in a desperate and terrifying voice: "I WANT MY BIG TOE!!!"

"Well, for the love of Moses, take it then!" the old woman said. "It's right there on the kitchen table!" And she rolled over one more time and tried to get some sleep.

Next morning the little old woman chuckled to herself about all the crazy dreams she'd had in the night. She went downstairs to boil the coffee, and there on the table, right where she had left it, set that canning jar with the lid screwed on tight.

The old woman picked it up for a closer look. But there was nothing in it. Not a pea-picking thing.

: Molly and Blunderbore :

You know how sisters are. Alike as peas in a pod, different as night and day. That was Molly and Poll all over.

Betts was off from home, staying with an old woman up on Granny's Branch. So that left just Molly and Poll at the house with Mommy and Poppy Whuppie. One morning they got to needing some water. But the water bucket was empty.

Well, they all knew they could dry up and die of thirst before Poll would ever go and draw water, so Molly Whuppie picked up the water bucket, and off she went to the well.

When she got there, she lowered the bucket down in the well, heard it fill with water glug glug glug, then commenced to pull it back up again. She was pulling and tugging and yanking on the rope, and somehow or another—don't ask me how—she fell in the well.

Down down down she dropped, through air and then water and then air again. Hit bottom and knocked herself out.

When she came to, she was in another world, and not knowing exactly what to do in the situation, Molly Whuppie got up and started walking down the road.

She walked and she walked, and she came to a log a-laying in the road. She was about to step on it and go on, when she thought she heard it speak.

"Walk around me, little gal," said the log. "Don't squash me down in the mud." So Molly walked around the log and went on.

Went on, went on, and she came to a sheep. Sheep could talk, too, in that world. "Shear me, little gal," said the sheep. "But not too close. For I need my woolly wool to keep me warm of a night." Molly sheared the sheep, but not too close, and continued on her way.

On and on and she came to an apple tree, and the apple tree spoke to her, too. "Pick you some apples to eat, little gal, but don't break my limbs off." Molly picked her some good apples to eat and was careful not to break any limbs.

Molly walked on till she came to a house. And what do you reckon she did then? Well, she marched right up to the door and knocked. And who do you reckon opened that door? A big hairy giant.

Well, she started to tell him about needing some water and falling in the well and getting knocked out and talking to a log and a sheep and a tree, but before she could get a word in, that giant whisked her in the house, set her down in a chair, and commenced to talk at her. He talked a blue streak. He talked her ears off. He talked till the cows came home. And all on just one topic—his own sweet self.

Well, that wouldn't have been so terrible bad if he hadn't been the most boring giant in seven counties and possibly the whole state. He was so boring it made Molly Whuppie want to run off and stick her head in the creek, just to get away from him.

And still he kept on talking. Molly dozed off a time or two. And still he kept on talking. And that's when Molly realized she'd dropped into the dwelling hole of Old Blunderbore.

Molly knew she had to get out of there quick or perish of boredom. Finally, in the middle of a very long and boring sentence, the giant stopped talking and began to snore. Molly slipped out of the house, trying not to make a sound for fear of rousting him.

Molly ran up the road just as hard as she could go. She looked back over her shoulder, and there he came after her, that big jaw still a-flapping. Molly ran till she got to the apple tree.

Now the apple tree knew all about Old Blunderbore and how tedious he was, and it told Molly, "Crawl up here in my limbs and hide." Molly climbed up in the apple tree limbs, so when the giant blundered by, he didn't see her and went and looked for her somewhere else.

Molly climbed down and went on, headed for the well and home. She got to the place where that sheep was grazing, and here came Old Blunderbore up on her again. The sheep knew all what was going on, too, and it told Molly, "Crawl up here in my woolly wool and hide." Molly crawled up in the sheep's wool and hid, so when the giant got there, he didn't see her that time either and stomped off in another direction.

Molly got out of there and went on, but before long she heard him after her again. She came to where that log was a-laying, and the log said, "Crawl in my holler and hide." Molly crawled in the holler of the log and hid, so when the giant came by, he never saw her.

Then Old Blunderbore's legs commenced to hurt him, from having to run all over the country first one way and then another, and him not used to that. So he went back to the house and laid down.

And what did Molly Whuppie do? Climbed up out of the well and went home.

Molly was tickled to see her mommy and daddy again, and they were tickled to see her, too. They thought she'd drowned in the well. She told them the whole story, and they made her tell it over and over while they rolled their eyes and slapped their knees and hollered, Law me! Do tell! If that don't beat all! and other similar expressions. They fixed Molly a big supper, let her have the best chair in the house, waited on her hand and foot, and just generally petted and made over her a sight.

Well, Poll, in the meantime, was over in the corner in a little hard chair, getting madder by the minute. "They're not paying a bit of atten-tion to me," she said to herself, since nobody else was listening. "And me the one that's been here the whole time while she was off on a spree." At first Poll was just a little bit peeved, but after while she worked herself up to where she was so mad she wanted to haul off and slap somebody.

About that time her mommy said, "Poll, go get Molly a piece of cake and a glass of buttermilk." Well, that did it right there. Poll couldn't stand it another minute. She tore out of there and went straight and jumped in the well.

Down down down she dropped, through air and then water and then air again. Hit bottom and knocked herself out.

When she came to, she was in another world, and not knowing what else to do in the situation, Poll got up and started walking down the road.

And she came to that log. "Walk around me, little gal," said the log. Well, Poll informed the log she was not about to be bossed by a piece of timber and would walk where she very well pleased. Poll plunked her big foot on the log and smooshed it way down in the mud.

Went on and she came to the sheep. "Shear me, little gal," said the sheep. "But not too close, for I need some woolly wool to keep me warm of a night." Poll sheared the sheep, all right, took all its wool and left it standing there a-shivering.

Went on and she got to the apple tree. "Get you some apples, little gal. But don't break my limbs off, please." Poll picked all the apples off the tree, broke its limbs off just for pure meanness, and went on down the road.

When Poll saw a house, she went and knocked on the door, and in a minute there before her stood Old Blunderbore. Well, when he saw she had ears on her head, he grabbed her and drug her in the house and made her set and listen to his mouth a-going till Poll thought she would lose her mind sure as the world.

Finally he dozed off and Poll slipped out of the house and tried to run off. But Old Blunderbore woke up and took out after her. Poll heard him coming and ran up to the apple tree hollering, "Hide me, hide me!"

"No limbs to hide you in," replied the tree.

Poll ran as fast as she could, the giant gaining on her by the second. She ran up to the sheep hollering, "Hide me, hide me!"

"No wool to hide you in," replied the sheep.

Poll kept running and she got to the log. "Hide me, hide me!" she begged.

"No holler to hide you in," replied the log. "My insides are all gommed up with mud."

Old Blunderbore caught up to Poll then, grabbed her and drug her kicking and screaming back to his house, where he set her back down in that same chair and commenced to tell her the whole history of the world, from Adam and Eve on down, what it all had to do with him personally, and all his opinions about it.

So there she set, trapped by her own jealousy and selfishness, not to mention the most boring giant in seven counties and possibly the whole state.

There she was, and there she stayed, till Molly Whuppie came and got her out.

: Molly Fiddler :

Things got droopy around the old homeplace, not too much a-going on. So Molly Whuppie up and decided she would go off and get her a job.

Well, she walked a big long way and she talked to a big lot of people and she still didn't have nary job. She was plumb give out and about to give up, when she spied a sign nailed to a gatepost. HEP WONTED, it read. Then in smaller letters at the bottom, NOK ON DORE.

So Molly Whuppie, being herself and nobody else, marched right up to the door of the house, bold as day, and knocked loud enough to raise the dead.

Come to find out a rich man lived there. He said if Molly would stay and work for him, he'd give her a sleeping room all to herself with a feather bed in it and all her eats besides.

Well, Molly Whuppie had never had a bed all to herself in her life. She had always had to sleep at the foot of the bed, and Poll and Betts were both bad to kick in their sleep. Tired and hungry as she was right then, that sounded pretty good, you know, a big soft feather bed and all she wanted to eat. So Molly Whuppie up and hollered, "I'll take it!" before a word was ever said about the pay.

But after she got in the bed that night she got to thinking, and she couldn't remember the giant saying anything at all about money. Did I mention he was a giant? Well, he was.

So first thing the next morning Molly asked him about her salary. A penny a year, the giant said. Molly said she was hoping to make a little more than that. But he said that was all he could afford, take it or leave it, so she took it.

Molly stayed and worked for that man a solid year and never got a payday, never even got the one penny. Stayed and worked another year, and never got a penny that time either. So after the third year she quit. Went and told the giant good-bye, I'm gone, I want my three cents.

Well, he tried ever way in the world to talk her out of leaving. He wanted her to stay there and work right on for nothing. Finally, when he saw she was bound and determined to go, he went and got the three pennies. Now he had enough money, that giant did, to burn two big wet mules. But he was tighter than the bark on a tree, and it just about killed him to have to turn loose of three cents.

Molly took her pennies and headed toward the county seat, thinking about the things she'd buy when she got to town. Molly never had been around money before, nor even been around anybody that had any, except the giant. So the whole world of finance was a mystery to her, and she had no more notion than a goose how much things cost. She figured she could buy a heap of things with three cents—a new hat, a horse and buggy, shoes, dresses, peppermint sticks—she had a big long list.

Well, she walked down the road a while and she met a young woman carrying a little child, and they stopped and spoke a minute. And the woman said to her, "Honey, I hate to beg, but have you got a penny you could let me have? My man's put me out, and I've got to get this baby something to eat."

"Why Lord yes," said Molly Whuppie. Handed the woman a penny, never thought a thing about it.

"I shore do thank ye," the woman said, and they parted ways.

Went a little further down the road and she met a feller, skinny as a fence rail, with clothes so raggedy, no self-respecting scarecrow would have been caught dead in them. And here he was out on the road, trying to get to his sister's house, and he didn't have a bite to eat either. Molly handed him a penny, and he thanked her and went on.

Molly walked a while longer, and there by the side of the road set a woman on a tree stump a-crying. So Molly went over there and asked her what the matter was.

"I'm about to get throwed out of my house," the woman said, "if I don't pay the landlord ever bit I owe him today, and I still lack one penny a-havin' it."

"Well, here's the penny," said Molly Whuppie, and she reached it out to her.

But the woman never took it, just smiled and said, "Maybe you better set here on the tree stump a minute, Molly. I've got news for you."

So they traded places. Then the woman said, "Molly Whuppie, I was sent here to test you. And you've been so good to me and the other people out on the road, I'm about to be good to you." Molly could have three wishes, she said, one for every penny she gave away.

Well, Molly Whuppie knew just exactly what she wanted. Many a night back home, she had laid at the foot of the bed, looking at the stars through the hole in the roof and planning what she would wish for if an opportunity like this came up.

"First, I wish for a slingshot," Molly Whuppie said, "that will hit anything I go to hit. Secondly, I wish I had a fiddle that when I go to play it, anybody that hears the music will commence to dance and cannot stop dancing as long as they hear that fiddle." Third, Molly wished for a new pair of shoes. The pair she had on were in a terrible shape.

The wish woman wasn't used to people asking for shoes, magic slingshots, and fiddles that made people dance whether they wanted to or not. But still a deal's a deal, and she thought she could just about manage it.

The wish woman told Molly Whuppie to set on the tree stump with her eyes closed and sing a big long ballad song and not leave out any verses. So Molly did. When she got to the end of the song and all the people in it were dead, Molly opened her eyes. The woman was gone, but there on the ground lay a slingshot, a new pair of shoes, and the prettiest fiddle you ever saw in your life, with a bow to go with it.

Molly put on her new shoes, picked up her tricks, and headed into town, where a big crowd was ganged up at the courthouse. Not the new courthouse, the old courthouse, the one that burned down. Everybody and their uncle was there, and their aunts and their cousins and their grandpas, too. And they were all whittling and spitting and preaching and politicking and waiting around to see some fellers get hung.

Molly went and joined a bunch of boys with rocks and slingshots. They were taking bets on who could hit a pine knot at the top of the courthouse. They didn't want to let Molly in on it at first, her being a girl and all, but you know Molly Whuppie. She would not be denied.

When it came her turn, all the boys bet against her. They figured she couldn't hit the side of a barn, let alone a pine knot. But they didn't know Molly Whuppie, and they didn't know her slingshot, either. Now Molly had a clear eye and a strong arm, even when she wasn't working with a magic slingshot, and when she was, well, she was mighty hard to beat.

Molly hit the pine knot spang in the middle ever time she drew back, so after while she had her a nice little pile of cash money. She got to feeling sorry for the boys and gave them some of it back.

Well, everybody was having a good old time till you-know-who showed up. That's right, Mr. Giant. Here he came into town, and when he saw the pile of money Molly had, it made him so mad he could not stand it. He hot-footed it straight to the sheriff's office and told the sheriff, who was kin to him two or three different ways, that he wanted Molly Whuppie put in jail right then or he wouldn't support him in the next election.

And then he stood right there and told a bald-faced lie. He claimed that Molly Whuppie had stole a big lot of money from him that morning, was down at the courthouse with it right then, and ought to be arrested for robbing, stealing, gambling, and having unladylike actions with a slingshot.

So the sheriff deputized the giant and everybody else that was standing around within deputizing distance, and they formed a posse to go arrest Molly Whuppie and put her in jail. When Molly saw them coming, she picked up her fiddle and she picked up her bow and commenced to burn 'em up on "Old Yaller Dog Come a-Trottin' through the Meetin' House."

Then all the people in town commenced to dance, even the ones that could not dance and the ones that did not believe in dancing and the ones that were about to get hung. And the sheriff and the giant and the posse, soon as that music hit their ears, linked up arms and began to dance, too, and such clogging, stomping, sashay-to-your-partner and do-si-do, well, you never saw the beat in your life.

They kept it up till way past dark, while Molly Whuppie, in the meantime, headed down the road and home, with her slingshot, her pile of money, her magic fiddle still a-playing, and her brand new pair of shoes.

: Runaway Cornbread :

Once upon a time there were three mice. They were not blind or anything, just regular mice, except they could talk and bake cornbread. Did they have names? Of course they did. Teddy, Taddy, and Little Redheaded Thing.

Well, they were all just mousing around at the house one day, and they got to wanting some cornbread to eat. But they didn't have any cornmeal to make it out of, just some corn they had grown, not yet ground into meal. So Teddy Mouse told Taddy Mouse to take the corn to the mill and have it ground. But Taddy stood in the middle of the floor and said, "No, I'll not do it. You ain't the boss of me."

Well, the fat was in the fire then. Teddy and Taddy lit in to quarreling. Teddy brought up everything Taddy had ever done that had made him mad, and Taddy named a long list of things Teddy did that got on his nerves.

While they stood there quarreling, Little Redheaded Thing took the corn to the mill and had it ground into meal. When she got back to the house, she built a fire in the cookstove, stirred up the cornbread, and slid it in the oven. And Teddy and Taddy still standing there fussing. But they left off when they smelled the cornbread baking and sat down at the table with their spoons in their hands, all ready to eat a big bait of crumble-in.

When the bread got good and brown, Little Redheaded Thing opened the oven door to pull it out. But before she could get it plumb out, that pone of cornbread jumped up OUT OF THE SKILLET and ran OUT THE DOOR and DOWN THE ROAD, with Teddy, Taddy, and Little Redheaded Thing chasing after it. Pone of Bread ran down the road till it came to a place where a man was grubbing newground. The man looked up and saw the pone of bread running down the road, and he asked it, said, "Where are ye running to, Pone of Bread?"

"I'm running away from Teddy Mouse, Taddy Mouse, and Little Redheaded Thing," replied Pone. Well, the man decided he'd a heap rather eat cornbread than grub newground, so he took out after the pone of bread, too, with his grubbing hoe still in his hand.

Pone of Bread ran down the road some more till it came to where a woman stood boiling clothes in a big black pot, beating them with a battling stick to get them clean. She never had seen a pone of bread in a big hurry like that before, and she asked it, said, "Where are ye running to, Pone of Bread?"

"I'm running from Teddy Mouse, Taddy Mouse, Little Redheaded Thing, and a man with a grubbing hoe," replied Pone. Now this woman had grown tired of her own cooking and wanted a bite of somebody else's, so she took out after the pone of bread, too, still holding on to that battling stick.

Pone of Bread ran down the road again till it came to a place where a boy was digging postholes. "Where are ye running to, Pone of Bread?" the boy wanted to know.

"I'm running from Teddy Mouse, Taddy Mouse, Little Redheaded Thing, a man with a grubbing hoe, and a woman with a battling stick." Well, just looking at cornbread made the boy hungry, so here he took off after it, too, dragging that big heavy posthole digger along with him.

Pone of Bread ran on down the road till it came to where a girl was out on the porch churning butter. "Where are ye running to, Pone of Bread?" she asked it.

"I'm running from Teddy Mouse, Taddy Mouse, Little Redheaded Thing, a man with a grubbing hoe, a woman with a battling stick, and a boy with a posthole digger." Well, that girl loved cornbread better than anything in this world. So she got up and took out after the pone of bread, too, and she brought her mommy's churn dasher with her.

Pone of Bread ran down the road some more, with Teddy, Taddy, Little Redheaded Thing, the man with the grubbing hoe, the woman with the battling stick, the boy with the posthole digger, and the girl with the churn dasher all running along behind it. The people that lived along the road all stepped out of their houses to watch, hollering, "See how they run!" and "Did you ever see such a sight in your life?" And they all swore and declared they never had.

Pone of Bread ran till it came to a high rock wall, and there it stopped. Pone could run, but climbing was a different matter. So it was just standing there trying to think what to do when over the hill burst that big rowdy crowd of people and mice, waving spoons and grubbing hoes and battling sticks and posthole diggers and churn dashers all in the air like weapons, and scared the poor little pone of cornbread half to death. So it jumped down in a hole in the ground and disappeared.

Then Teddy Mouse and Taddy Mouse and the man with the grubbing hoe and the woman with the battling stick and the boy with the post-hole digger and the girl with the churn dasher all got mad and upset because they had lost their cornbread. And they started arguing amongst themselves over whose cornbread it was to begin with and who should have got the biggest piece if they had caught it and whose fault it was they didn't catch it and now it was gone.

Inside of five minutes they were in the awfullest ruckus ever was, their faces red as beets, yelling, stomping, swinging farm tools and other domestic implements around ever which away in a most alarming manner.

Well, while all that was a-going on, Little Redheaded Thing just turned around and went back to the house. She got some corn out of the corncrib, took it to the mill and had it ground, brought it back to the house and made it into bread, put it in the oven (which was still hot from a while ago), and went out and sat in the porch swing while it baked.

When it got good and brown, Little Redheaded Thing pulled the cornbread out of the oven. Plumb out this time. Set it on the table and sat down and ate it. Ate the whole thing right by herself, the way I heard the tale. And that, my dears, was the end of that.

Molly & the Ogre Who Would Not Pick Up

One day Polly Whuppie was out behind the house when a little blue ball came floating by, right in the middle of the air. It was about the size of an apple but blue, blue as a robin's egg, and it sparkled like sunlight on water. So Poll just naturally followed it.

She followed it, but she never could quite catch it, for it stayed always just beyond her reach and drew her ever deeper into the dark woods.

Now in the dark woods was a deep hole in the ground, and in that hole dwelled the Untidy Ogre, who never cleared his place after supper, never took the garbage out, and threw his dirty socks just anywhere. And what was worse, he kept women as his prisoners down there and forced them to cook, house-clean, and do big washings and ironings for him.

After the women got down there, they didn't know how to get out again, and they were just miserable. There was a big lot of screaming and crying went on down there, as you might imagine. And that is the situation in which Poll found herself.

Well, Molly and Betts, in the meantime, did not know what in the world had become of Poll. Every day they went out and looked for her. Molly would go one way and Betts the other.

One day when they were out looking, Betts spied a little blue ball a-floating, too. And she just naturally followed it, and it drew her ever deeper into the dark woods, and she fell down in the ogre's den and had to start picking up after him also.

So then Molly Whuppie had to try and find both her sisters. She searched for a year and a month and a week and a day, but she found no trace.

One day she got so down and discouraged, not knowing what to do nor where to turn, that she sat down by the side of the road and busted out a-crying. Suddenly an old woman appeared out of nowhere, and she asked Molly, said, "What's the matter with you?"

"My sisters are gone and I don't know what's become of them," Molly blubbered. She dried her eyes on her apron and looked at the old woman. "Are you a witch?" Molly asked.

At first the woman looked like she might be insulted. Then she laughed. "A witch? Law, no! I'm a poet, honey. But so many people have asked me that question, I wrote a poem about it, which I happen to have on my person. Would you like to hear it?"

Molly was trying to think of a polite way to say, "No, thank you, I'm not much in the mood for poetry," or something to that effect, but by that time the old woman was well into the second stanza:

Just because I choose not to wear makeup
Just because I don't carry a purse
Try to go your own way, try to have your own say
They will call you a witch or worse.

Just because you may have certain powers
Just because you have found your own niche
They'll assume you have prisoners in towers
And your son is the son of a witch.

So she has a few hairs on her chin
So she doesn't go ga-ga for men
So she has a sharp nose
She likes wearing black clothes

And a tall pointy hat.
Tell me, what's wrong with that?
They'll stub their big toe and declare it's a curse.
They'll call you a witch or worse.

Well, Molly didn't know what to say after all that, so she just didn't say anything, which was probably the best course. The old woman put the poem back in her pocket and in its place came up with a silver needle and a spool of gold thread, which she handed to Molly.

"Thank you," Molly said, but to tell the truth she was a little disappointed. She was hoping for something more useful. "Is that all?" she asked.

"That and this," the old woman replied, and before anybody could stop her she began to recite another poem:

Gold and silver, sun and sea
Love and courage set them free.

And then she was gone. And so Molly went on her way, ever closer to the ogre's dark den. And she found it the only way she could, by falling in it herself.

Molly got up, dusted herself off, and went and knocked on the ogre's door. When it opened, there he stood. Molly had thought he would be terrible looking, but he wasn't. In fact, he seemed to change before her very eyes, a handsome gentleman one minute, Bossy Untidy Ogre the next.

"I believe you've got my sisters here, sir," Molly said. "I've come to fetch 'em, and I won't leave here without 'em."

"You won't leave here at all," replied the ogre, and he reached out to grab her. But instead he got a silver needle jobbed in the palm of his hand and a poem spoke in his ear:

Gold and silver, sun and sea
Love and courage set them free.

The ogre seemed not to like the poem nor the needle either, and he pushed Molly down on the floor. While she was down there, Molly noticed the ogre was barefoot, and she took her needle and commenced to job him in the foot with it, which caused him to fall down on the floor and beg her to quit.

Molly tied him up good and tight with the gold thread. Then she ran all over the house, opening all the doors and letting out all the women that the ogre had held prisoner. They all threw down their brooms and

Molly & the Ogre Who Would Not Pick Up : : : 37

dust rags and scouring pads and ran out of there singing, dancing, and playing musical instruments, leaving the Untidy Ogre to pick up after himself.

Among the women Molly saw her own dear sisters, Poll and Betts. And they were all so pleased to find one another again that they laughed and cried and hugged and talked all at the very same time and went with their arms across one another's shoulders all the way home.

: Pig Tale :

Once upon a time, a long time ago, there lived an old woman, and this old woman lived in a house, and the house sat beside a creek, and the creek had a little wooden footbridge over it, which the old woman walked across on her way to wherever she was going.

Since the old woman lived alone, she had nobody to help her with the housework, and so she had to do it all herself. And she got sick and tired of it. She got so sick and tired of it, in fact, doing the same chores day after day after blessed day, that one day, she up and quit.

She stopped mopping. She swore off sweeping. She would not even look at a dust rag. She sat and rocked in her rocking chair while the dishes piled up in the dishpan and the garbage piled up by the door.

Well, it was not long till she was in the worst mess ever was. Finally it got so bad she couldn't stand it anymore. "I am living in a pig sty!" the old woman declared, and she lit in to cleaning. She rubbed and scrubbed and dubbed. She swept and swabbed and mopped and flopped. And she found things. Three smelly socks, no two alike. A shriveled-up apple, which she ate anyway. A comb she had accused her sister of stealing. And a silver dollar.

"I know just exactly what I aim to do with YOU!" the old woman said, addressing the silver dollar. And she took that silver dollar, headed down the road with it, and did not stop till she came to a sign that read PIGS FOR SALE. The old woman had been wanting a pig for the longest time.

"Do you have any pigs today?" she demanded of the farmer at the gate.

"I should hope to kiss a pig I do!" replied the farmer, and he went right then to fetch one.

And here he came back with it. No pig in a poke, either. But the pinkest, plumpest, prettiest, most perfect pig in all the long proud history of pigs. "Now *that* is a pig!" the farmer bragged. And the old woman had to agree. It was a pig, all right.

"I'll take it!" she said, and the trade was made.

"Don't rush off," said the farmer. "Stay for supper."

"No, thank you," the old woman answered. "I've got to get home before dark."

And so she headed back up the road toward home, singing "Pig in a Pen" just as loud as she could sing, with her silver-dollar pig trotting smartly along behind her.

Well, everything went smooth as silk till they got to the little wooden footbridge. The old woman walked on over the bridge. The pig, however, did not. The pig just sat there, still as a stump, staring at the shaky little footbridge and the rushing water beneath. The pig had a thing about water.

"Come on, Pig Head!" the old woman demanded.

"Not by the hair of my chinny chin chin," thought the pig.

"You cross this bridge right now!" the old woman ordered.

"When pigs fly," thought the pig.

"You cross this bridge or I'll turn you into souse and sausage before you can say pickled pigs' feet!" the old woman warned.

"Pickled pigs' feet," thought the pig.

"I do not know why I am standing here talking to a pig," the old woman decided. So she tried pushing it instead. Next she tried pulling, and then picking up. But pulling worked no better than pushing, and picking up did not work at all, for push, pull, or pick up, that pig stayed put.

Well, the old woman saw she would never get the pig over the bridge by herself. So she headed back down the road toward the pig farm to try to find some help. And she came to a stick a-laying in the road.

And she said to the stick, "Stick," said she, "I want you to poke that pig and prod that pig on over that bridge. For I've got to get home before dark."

"I'd prefer not to," said the stick.

"Mighty picky for a stick," the old woman grumbled. And she walked on down the road till she came to a fire burning.

And she said to the fire, "Fire," said she, "I want you to burn that stubborn stick. For the stick won't poke the pig, the pig won't cross the bridge, and I've got to get home before dark!"

"I'd rather not," replied the fire.

The old woman walked on, mad as fire, till she came upon a puddle of water in the road.

And she said to the water, "Water," said she, "I want you to quench that good-for-nothing fire. For the fire won't burn the stick, the stick won't poke the pig, the pig WILL NOT cross the bridge, and I've got to get home before dark!"

"Well, I might," replied the water. "Then again, I might not."

"Thanks for nothing," the old woman snorted, and she went on till she met a mule.

And she said to the mule, "Mule," said she, "I wish you would drink that wishy-washy water. For the water won't quench the fire, the fire won't burn the stick, the stick won't poke the pig, the pig FLAT REFUSES to cross the bridge, and I've got to get home before dark!"

"I'm not thirsty," brayed the mule.

The old woman threw up her hands, walked on, and came to a rope coiled up.

And she said to the rope, "Rope," said she, "I want you to lasso that mean mule. For the mule won't drink the water, the water won't quench the fire, the fire won't burn the stick, the stick won't poke the pig, the pig FOR LOVE NOR MONEY won't cross the bridge, and I've got to get home before dark!"

But the rope was not in a lassoing mood.

On and on, and she met a mouse. And she said to the mouse, "Mouse," said she, "I want you to gnaw that moody rope. For the rope won't lasso the mule, the mule won't drink the water, the water won't quench the fire, the fire won't burn the stick, the stick won't poke the pig, the pig TO SAVE THE WORLD won't cross that bridge, and I've got to get home before dark!"

"No, thank you," squeaked the mouse. "I'm trying to cut down."

On she went and she met a cat. And she said to the cat, "Cat," said she, "I want you to chase that uncooperative mouse. For the mouse won't gnaw the rope, the rope won't lasso the mule, the mule won't drink the water, the water won't quench the fire, the fire won't burn the stick, the stick won't poke the pig, ONE THOUSAND ARMIES COULDN'T MAKE THAT PIG GO OVER THAT BRIDGE, and I've got to get home before dark!"

Have you ever tried to get a cat to do anything? Enough said.

The old woman stomped down the road and she met a dog. And she opened her mouth to say, "Dog, I want you to get that cat, for the cat won't chase the mouse, the mouse won't gnaw the rope, the rope won't lasso the mule, the mule won't drink the water, the water won't quench the fire, the fire won't burn the stick, the stick won't poke the pig, the pig won't cross the bridge, and I've got to get home before dark."

But before she could actually say that, the dog spied the cat and took out after it. So the cat, to save its life, ran away in the direction of the mouse. The mouse saw it coming and hid behind the rope, which it began to gnaw upon nervously. And the rope, to get away from the mouse, rose up in the air and came down around the mule's neck, which caused the mule to feel thirsty and start drinking the water. That made the water slosh up and start putting out the fire, and the fire flared up and started burning the stick, so the stick popped out of the fire and started poking the pig. And the pig, SUDDENLY OVERCOMING ITS FEAR OF WATER, trotted on over the bridge and home, crying "Wee Wee Wee" all the way.

"Well, if that don't beat a hog a-flying," said the old woman, who made it home before dark after all. Which was a good thing, because there was her boyfriend, waiting on the porch. It seems they had a date that night.

And ever after that day, the old woman and her boyfriend and her pig lived happy and peaceful. Happy as a hog with a bucketful of slop. Peaceful as a pig in a puddle.

: Molly and the Unwanted Boyfriends :

The seasons kept going round, and the sun kept coming up and going down like always. And the Whuppies went to sleep and woke up again and ate their meals and did their work and lived their lives like everybody else. And different things happened to them, some good and others not so good, but they kept on living just the same, and the time kept going by. And Molly Whuppie got to be a great big girl.

And one day she went and asked her mommy and daddy didn't they reckon it was time for her to go off from home and live and do by her own self.

Well, no, they didn't reckon that a-tall. Molly was their baby, and they wanted her to stay right there with them all her life or else marry a boy from up the road. So when Molly started packing her tricks to go, they went all to pieces. They cried and carried on, bawled and bellowed and boo-hoo-hooed, got back in the bed and wouldn't get out, swore they were a-dying or at least real bad off sick.

But when they saw Molly had her mind made up and that all that carrying on was not doing one bit of good, they crawled out of bed, gave her what little money they had, which was not much, and let her go.

Now Molly Whuppie never was one of these nervous types of persons that go around with a hanky in their hand and won't stay by themselves of a night and won't walk past the graveyard after dark, afraid the booger-man will get them. Molly located her a little house up on Whippoorwill Branch and moved in it right by herself. And she got along just fine.

Well, there also lived on Whippoorwill at that time three young men, brothers, all bachelors, never had been married. And when they got the news Molly Whuppie had moved in nearby, they washed their feet, slicked back their hair, and headed up the creek to visit.

Well, that would have been all right, I guess, but the sad case was that not one of them boys had a lick of sense, and if they had they wouldn't have known what to do with it. And still yet, for reasons nobody knows nor understands to this day, they were all three so stuck on themselves and so big in the head it was all they could do to squeeze through the door.

Molly Whuppie pretty quick saw how things stood, and she told all three of the boys, plain as she could, that she'd be their friend but she would not put up with anything in the way of courting. Well, they were just big old rough boys and their listening skills were highly undeveloped, and so they kept right on just like she never had said that.

One evening Molly was sitting on the couch stringing beans when one of the boys showed up, uninvited, and plopped himself down on the couch, too. Directly he eased over toward Molly and started trying to kiss her. She told him to quit, but he wouldn't quit. "Oh sugar," he said, "why won't you let me kiss you?"

"All right, you can kiss me," Molly said. "But first you'll have to get up and lock the door." So he got up to lock the door, and just as he took a-holt of the knob Molly said, "You grab hit, and hit grabs you."

Well, he found out he couldn't turn loose of the doorknob. Molly Whuppie went to bed and slept all night, and he had to stand there with the doorknob in his hand till daylight broke and turned him loose. Then he took out of there like a house afire and never did come back.

The next night Molly was sitting hulling peas when the second brother showed up, completely unannounced. He flopped himself down on the couch, and directly he sidled over toward Molly and started trying to kiss her. And she told him, "Quit that!" But he wouldn't quit. "Oh sugar, oh honey," he said, "why won't you let me kiss you?"

Molly said, "All right, you can kiss me, but first you'll have to get up and cover the fire with ashes." So he got up to cover the fire with ashes, and when he took a-holt of the shovel Molly said, "You grab hit, and hit grabs you."

Well, he found out he couldn't move and he couldn't turn loose of the shovel. Molly hit the hay and slept sound all night, and he had to stand there with the shovel in his hand till daylight broke and let him go. He took off like he'd seen a ghost and never did come back.

Well, the next night Molly was husking corn and the third brother came in on her, unannounced and uninvited both, sot himself down on the couch, scrooched over, and commenced a-trying to kiss. "Quit that!" Molly told him, but he wouldn't quit.

"Oh sugar, oh honey, oh molasses candy, why won't you let me kiss you?" he said.

"All right, you can kiss me," Molly told him. "But first you'll have to get up and put out the cat." So he got up and got the cat. "You grab hit, and hit grabs you," Molly said, and he couldn't move and couldn't let go of the cat.

Molly hit the shucks and slept good all night, and the feller had to stand there holding that cat till daylight broke and let him go. He took off like the law was after him, and he never did come back either.

So that was the end of the trouble with the unwanted boyfriends. But that's just one story about Molly Whuppie. I could write a book about her.

: Grind Mill Grind :

Once there lived two brothers, one rich and the other poor. The rich brother had everything a person could need in this world and more—a big fine home, a horse and buggy, a thousand acres of good bottom-land, and a big gang of people to work it for him.

But the other brother, he didn't have much of anything at all. He lived in a little old falling-down house in a rocky corner of the rich brother's land. Every day he worked sunup to sundown for his brother. And every night his brother would give him just barely enough food for him and his wife to get by on. Years and years went by like that. The poor one couldn't get ahead. The only thing he was ahead of was starvation, and not much ahead of that.

Well, Christmastime was coming, and it was a real bad winter, real cold, a big snow on the ground, worst time ever was. Naturally there wasn't much work to do on the rich brother's farm, right in the middle of the frozen winter like that. So the poor brother had no way to get his eats.

Well, it got to be Christmas Eve, and the poor brother went to the rich brother's house and asked him, said, "Brother, we've got nothing to eat at our house for Christmas. Could you spare us some meat to eat?" And he promised he'd work it out when the weather broke.

Well, the way the rich brother quarreled and carried on, you'd have thought somebody was trying to take everything that he had. Finally he sent to the smokehouse for a ham. Handed it to his brother, told him to go on home and not ask for anything else. And a Merry Christmas to him.

The poor brother thanked him, wished him a Merry Christmas back, and started home with his ham. It was good and dark by then, a cold keen wind a-blowing, and the snow just pouring down. It was hard to see, but the poor man knew his way back home. Or he thought he did.

He had to go through a patch of woods to get there. He'd gone that way a thousand times, but this night he got in that patch of woods and got turned around some way or another and got lost. Looked around and everything looked strange to him. He didn't know where he was nor which way to go, so he just kept walking.

He began to hear a sound far off, like somebody chopping wood, and he started toward that sound. It led him finally to a cabin and an old man out front a-chopping wood. So he went up to the man and said, "Merry Christmas, friend. Can you tell me where I'm at? I have messed around out here in this snow and got lost."

The old man put down his ax. "You've blundered into goblin territory," he said. "And if they see that ham, they're liable to take it away from you. For the goblins love ham meat better than anything on earth. I expect they'll smell it in a minute and be out here after it."

"Lord, I hope not," the poor man said. "For this ham is all in the world I've got for Christmas dinner."

"I'll tell you what to do," the woodcutter said. "A goblin will bargain and trade. They're in the cabin there right now. Go in there and say you'll swap them the ham for their little mill that stands behind the door. Then bring the mill out here, and I'll show you how to work it."

The poor brother said, "Well, I thank you, but I need this ham to eat a lot more than I need a mill."

"If you had that mill," the woodcutter told him, "you wouldn't have to worry about anything to eat."

The poor brother went and knocked on the goblins' door. It opened a crack, and in two shakes of a sheep's tail those goblins were all over that ham.

The poor brother held the ham as high as he could over his head. "Now hold your horses, little fellers," he said. "I'll let ye have the ham, but you'll have to give me something in trade. I'll take that little old mill that stands behind the door."

Well, the goblins didn't much want to give him their mill, but they wanted the ham so bad, they finally agreed. The poor brother got the mill and took it back outside. It looked like nothing but an ordinary little hand mill, one you might use to grind sausage with, and a rusty little old mill at that. The poor man wondered if he hadn't just been rooked out of his Christmas ham by a crafty woodcutter and a gang of goblins.

"This mill will grind out anything in the world you want," the woodcutter said. "Except ham. It won't grind out ham. But anything else you want, just crank the handle and say, 'Grind mill grind.'" To make it quit, he told him to turn the handle backward and say:

Mind well grind mill
That stood behind the door
Mind well mill will
Grind no more.

The poor brother thanked him, took the mill, and quicker than you can blink your eye he was back at his own house.

"Where in the world have you been?" his old woman wanted to know, soon as he stepped in the door. "I've set here the livelong night, worried to death, and not a bite to eat in the house. And what's that rusty old mess you've drug in here on me?"

"Hush a minute and I'll show you," he said, and he asked her what she wanted to eat.

"I been studying about ham all day," she said.

"Well, study about something else," he told her.

She reckoned, upset as she was, she might could force down a little dab of turkey and dressing. And shuck beans and soup beans. Some corn pudding, maybe. And blackberry cobbler, she might could eat that.

The poor brother turned the handle and spoke the words. "Grind mill grind," he said, and the mill started grinding out turkey and dressing and every kind of food the woman named. He had to hurry up and stop it before it ground out too much. Then they sat down and had the biggest Christmas dinner they ever had in their lives.

Next day they ground out fried chicken. Next day something else. Next day something else. Every day they started up the mill and ground out everwhat they wanted to eat.

Then they got to asking the mill to grind out good clothes for them to wear and new house plunder, and it ground out that. Then the man, he would say the right words, and the mill would quit. They ground out money, big sacks full of it, more than they would ever need in their lives.

So the man, he didn't have to work for his brother anymore. And his brother noticed it and came around to see what the matter was, why he hadn't been to work.

"I don't have to work for you no more," he told him, said, "I've got me a mill now." And he was so proud of it, he got it out and showed his brother how it worked.

Well, as soon as the rich brother saw that mill he had to have it. But his brother didn't aim to sell. They went around and around about it till finally the one with the mill saw that his brother would never leave till he got what he wanted, so he said all right, he'd sell it to him for two thousand dollars and one-fourth of the rich brother's land.

The rich brother said all right, he'd trade that way, and he took the mill and went on back to his house. Didn't tell his wife a thing about it. Next morning he asked her, said, "Why don't you go up to your sister's this morning? I'll cook dinner and have it ready when you get back."

Well, she was well pleased with that idea. He never would do anything around the house like that before. He asked her what she wanted to eat, and she said she was in a mood to eat fish and gravy. Then she went up to her sister's and left him there to cook. He got the mill out, cranked the handle, and said "Grind mill grind." Told it to grind out fish and gravy, and it started grinding out fish and gravy. Ground out a big mess, a lot more than they'd eat for their dinner, just them two. So he told it to quit, said, "Quit, mill. Quit grinding fish and gravy now." He'd forgot the right words to say to make it quit.

So the mill kept right on grinding out fish and gravy. He filled up every pot vessel in the house with fish and gravy, and still the fish kept flopping and the gravy kept glopping.

Well, the man soon saw he'd have to get out of there or else be drowned in gravy. He opened the front door and the gravy roared out like a dam busting. He made a beeline for his brother's house to get him to come and stop the mill.

Meanwhile, his wife had started back home from her sister's house, and who should she meet but her husband a-running down the road with a big wall of fish and gravy right behind him. "Lord have mercy!" she hollered, and she fell down flat on the ground, sure that the end of time had come at last.

Her man never stopped to explain, just ran on as quick as he could to his brother's house, with fish and gravy spreading out over the fields like a springtime flood. He called out his brother, said, "Come and shut this dang thing off before it destroys everything in the country."

His brother came out there and said, "Now let's not get overexcited. Set down and relax and tell me what the trouble is."

The other one hollered, "No, I'll not set down! You've got to come right now and help me!"

"Well, brother, they's a heap of things in life easier to start than they are to stop, and this mill is one of them. What will you give me to turn it off?"

"Anything!"

"Well, I might could do it, but I'd have to have another two thousand dollars and another one-fourth of your land."

"Take it! Just stop the mill!"

So he turned the handle backward and said the right words:

Mind well grind mill
That stood behind the door
Mind well mill will
Grind no more.

The mill quit grinding then, and everything settled down. Every man, woman, child, dog, and cat in the county had fish and gravy for supper that night. Except the rich brother. He said he never wanted to see fish and gravy again as long as he lived.

So after that the poor brother wasn't so poor anymore. The rich brother wasn't so rich, and he wasn't so greedy, either. Ever since that close call with the fish and gravy, he was a changed man.

I don't know if it's the truth, but I heard tell he sold the mill to a storekeeper that traveled all over the world buying merchandise to bring back and sell at his store. And one time the storekeeper was away out on the ocean on his ship, and he had the little mill with him. He was eating him a mess of fish he'd caught, and he needed a pinch of salt to go with it. So he told that mill to grind out salt. Well, it ground out salt and it ground out salt and it ground out salt some more. Finally he told it to stop.

"All right, you can stop grinding out salt now," he said. He'd forgot the right words, too, and the mill kept right on grinding.

Well, they tried everything but the right thing to make it stop and it wouldn't. It ground out so much salt it was about to sink the ship. So to save their lives they had to take and throw the mill overboard, and it was still grinding salt as it sank beneath the waves. And as far as I know it is grinding still yet, somewhere down at the bottom of the sea. And that, as anybody will tell you, is why ocean water tastes like salt.

: Jack and the Christmas Beans :

Winter was coming on strong, and Jack was living up at the head of the holler with his mommy and his poppy and his brothers Will and Tom. And they were poor, poor as Job's turkey.

And speaking of turkeys, they were not likely to have one for Christmas dinner. In fact, they were not likely to have much of anything at all. All the garden truck they had put up in the summer was gone. No more meat in the meat box. No more jars in the cellar. No more sweet taters in the sweet tater hole. No money and no way to get any.

Then to beat it all, three days before Christmas, the cow went dry. Next the well went dry. And the hen, seeing how things were going, got so down and discouraged she couldn't lay one more egg.

"Don't look for Christmas to come this year," Pap told the boys. "Not to this house."

Well, naturally Will and Tom and Jack couldn't stand the thoughts of that for one minute. So they got busy and lit in to thinking. They thought so hard and so long and so fast, they felt that their heads must surely bust wide open. Finally they came up with a plan.

"Now the way I see it," Tom began, in a professorial manner, "if Christmas won't come to our house, then we'll just have to go out and fetch it!"

"We'll hunt Christmas and haul it back here!" agreed Will.

"Let's head for the North Pole first thing in the morning!" Jack put in.

"It's brilliant!" said Will.

"It's foolproof!" said Tom.

"It's clever and cunning!" said Jack.

"It's the stupidest plan I ever heard in my life," said Pap, who was listening at the door. Pap tried his best to talk the boys out of going. But Mam said he was wasting his breath and started in baking journey cakes.

The boys went to bed early that night so they could wake up good and rested in the morning and carry out their plan. But Will and Tom had a plan of their own. They'd sneak off and go without Jack.

"He's too little to go," Will told Tom.

"He's too silly to go," Tom told Will. But really they just wanted to keep all the presents for themselves.

The next morning, two days before Christmas, Will and Tom got up before daylight, slipped around real quiet, and pulled out for the North Pole. Left Jack asleep in the bed.

Will and Tom walked and walked till they walked so far they came to a place they never had been to before. And still they kept on walking. Finally they met an old man.

"Have you boys got ary thing to eat?" the old man asked them. "I'm about starved to death."

"Sorry, old uncle," said Will. "We ain't got enough for our own selves."

"And we've no time to fool with you," added Tom. "We're leaving this country, headed north." And they left the old man standing there just as hungry as he had been before.

Will and Tom walked on, walked on, and it got up late in the day. Directly the sun eased down behind the mountain, and it set in cold, cold as kraut.

Walked on and they met an old woman. And that woman had no coat on, just a little old raggedy dress and carrying an empty basket on her arm. She was so cold she was blue.

"Will one of you good boys give me your coat to wear a minute?" she asked them. "I'm about froze to death."

"Sorry, old sister," said Will. "We'll be needing our coats such a night as this."

"And we've no time to fool with you," added Tom. "We're out on important Christmas business."

So on they walked, and along about dark they came to a wilderness place. Not a light, not a house, not a soul in sight. Will and Tom had already eaten all their journey cakes, and even with their coats on, they were so cold their teeth clattered in their heads. Neither one said it, but they were both having second thoughts about the plan.

Then they spied something coming down the road. They'd seen nothing like it before in their lives and had no earthly notion what it might be. Whatever it was, it was big as a haystack, white as the snow, and headed right at them.

Will's and Tom's eyes got big as saucers. They turned tail and took out of there just as hard as they could go, yelling and hollering every step of the way, and did not stop till they got back home, where they jumped in the bed and pulled the covers up over their pointy little heads.

Next morning, the day before Christmas, Jack woke up and told his mommy, said, "Well, I reckon I'll head on up to the North Pole." She packed his journey cakes for him, and Jack put on his old raggedy coat and lit out.

Jack walked and walked till he walked so far he came to a place he'd never been to before. And he met that old man.

"Jack, have you got anything to eat?" the old man asked him. "I'm about starved—"

"Why, shore!" said Jack, and he pulled out the journey cakes. "It's not much, but you're welcome to it."

Jack and the old man sat on a log by the side of the road and ate their journey cakes. They talked and laughed, told tales, sang songs, and generally had them a big old time.

"Jack, you've been good to me," the old man said, "and I want to give you a present." He reached down in his britches pocket then and pulled out three little bean seeds. "Christmas beans," he said.

Well, Jack couldn't wait to see how a Christmas bean worked. He scratched a hole in the ground, dropped in a bean, and covered it with dirt.

"Jump back!" the old man hollered.

Jack jumped back, and just in the nick of time, too, for from that seed there shot up out of the ground the biggest prettiest Christmas tree you ever saw in your life. Presents grew on that tree like apples and fell off on the ground.

Jack and the old man played with the presents till Jack remembered he was going somewhere. Jack thanked the old man and walked on down the road till he met the woman with no coat on and the empty basket on her arm.

"Jack, will you let me wear your coat a minute?" she asked him. "I'm about froze—"

"Why, shore!" said Jack, and he pulled off his coat. "It's not much, but you're welcome to it."

The old woman put on Jack's coat. After while, she got to where she wasn't quite so blue, and she said, "Jack, you've been good to me, and I want to give you a present." And she handed Jack her basket.

"Whenever you want anything to eat," she told him, "just take this basket and say, 'Fill, basket, fill.'"

Well, Jack couldn't wait to see how that worked, either. "Fill, basket, fill!" Jack said, and a big ham jumped out. Then pickled beets, deviled eggs, chicken and dumplings, cornbread and biscuits, a dried apple stack cake, and two or three chocolate pies.

Jack and the old woman sat on a rock and had them a feast. They talked and laughed, told tales, sang songs, and danced a Christmas jig in the middle of the road. Had the best time ever was. Finally Jack said, well, he better go if he was to make the Pole before dark.

Walked on, walked on all that evening, and he came to a wilderness place. Not a light, not a house, not a soul in sight. Jack walked on, and directly he seen it a-coming, a gollywhopper of a thing, big as a haystack, white as the snow, and headed right at him.

"I can't wait to see what that is," said Jack, and he walked toward it faster. The next thing Jack knew he was standing there looking at a BIG WHITE . . . bear, which shook Jack's hand with a furry paw and said, "Merry Christmas, Jack."

"Merry Christmas, Bear," Jack said back. "What are you doing out such a cold dark night?"

"What do you reckon I'm a-doing?" said the bear. "I'm looking for somebody to spend Christmas Eve with."

"Look no more," said Jack. "You have found your man."

Jack and the bear climbed up the mountain to the bear's cave and built them a big good fire. About midnight, Jack held out his basket. "Fill, basket, fill!" said Jack. Then he pulled out a Christmas bean. "Jump back!" Jack hollered to the bear.

Jack and the bear stayed up all night, telling big tales, playing games, singing songs, dancing, making music, and just generally having them a spree right there in the cave. Then they went outside.

It was a clear night, the sky full of stars, which looked so close and shone so bright, Jack thought he could reach out and touch one.

Jack thought it, and the bear did it. Reached up, pulled down a star, and tucked it, still warm, into the palm of Jack's hand.

"You're good company, Jack," said the bear, "but maybe you ought to go home for Christmas, to your mommy and your poppy and your brothers Will and Tom. They'll be a-missin' ye."

Jack knew the bear talked sense. So he packed up his star, his basket, and his bean and started down the road toward home.

"Hold up a minute, Jack!" called the bear. "I'll give ye a lift."

Before you could say "Merry Christmas," Jack was sitting on the soft strong back of the bear. Before you could say "Happy New Year," they were flying through the sky, just as the sun popped up on Christmas morning.

The bear came in for a landing about a mile down the road from Jack's house. Jack didn't want his mommy and poppy to look up and see him flying in on a bear's back and be asking him a big lot of questions about it.

Mam and Pap were so tickled to see Jack, they didn't care how he'd got home nor whether he'd found Christmas. Will and Tom were not so generous, however.

"Where's Christmas at, Jack?" Will wanted to know.

"All I see is an empty basket," said Tom.

"Fill, basket, fill," said Jack.

Jack pulled out that last Christmas bean. "Jump back!" he hollered.

And didn't they all have a big time then, playing games, telling tales, dancing, singing, making music, eating all their food, and opening all their presents.

Jack let the others have the presents, and he played with the star he got from the bear. Jack had everything he needed and more and was well satisfied.

If Jack ever made it to the North Pole, I never did hear about it. Things don't always go just like you plan them. And you don't always find a thing the first place you think to look. And I reckon that's all right. For Pole or no Pole, Jack found Christmas.

: Molly and Jack :

One time Molly Whuppie was going down the road hunting for a job when she spied a big fine house set back from the road. She felt sorry for the people who lived there, having to keep up a big place like that, and she thought she might help them out. So she went and knocked on the door, and who should appear but a big old giant.

"What in the world do YOU want?" That's what he said. No "Howdy," "Nice weather," "Kiss my foot," or nothing. Just "What in the world do YOU want?" And not in the pleasantest of tones either.

Molly told him she was out job hunting. "Well, I can give you a job," said the giant. "Hit's hard work and low pay. I'm the boss, and you have to do just what I tell you and not say a word about it." Molly said yeah, she knew what a job was. So she stayed and worked around the giant's place.

And she got along all right, Molly did. She could make do in about any situation and not get bad downhearted about it. She could always find something to do that needed doing, she said, or something to think on that pleased her.

The giant kept horses, and Molly liked that, especially this one horse named Raglif Jaglif Tartliff Pole. She'd slip off and ride him and talk to him every chance she got.

But it was lonesome up there. That giant had a bad name in the community, and the people had got afraid to come around him. But one day a young feller showed up, and Molly heard him and the giant talking out on the porch. The boy said he was out job hunting, too. Said his name was Jack.

"Well, Mr. Jack, will you work?" the giant asked him.

"Law yes, I'll work," Jack said back. "I'm the workinest man ever was. Just give me any old job, and I'll do it the best in the world."

"Is that so?" said the giant. "Well, that being the case, Mr. Jack, I've got a job for you, and we'll just see how well you do. I've got a barn down here that's not been cleaned out in seven years. I'm about to go to town here in a minute. If you can get that barn cleaned out by the time

I get back, I'll give you a big sack of money. If you can't, I'll have to cut your head off."

Well, anybody would rather have a big sack of money than their head cut off, so naturally Jack was a little uneasy about that part of the arrangement. But he didn't want to say anything negative and risk being branded a troublemaker his first day on the job. So he said, well, all right.

The giant took Jack out to the barn, showed him an old shovel, a new shovel, and a big mountain of manure. Told him, "Git busy." Said he'd be back about dark.

Jack took the new shovel and lit in trying to clean out that barn. There was a sight of manure in there, and to make matters worse, every time Jack pitched one shovelful out, two more shovelfuls would come back in. After while there was so much more manure than there had been to start with that Jack began to feel discouraged. But he kept right on bravely shoveling anyhow, and he might have been there shoveling yet if Molly Whuppie hadn't come out to check on him.

"How you getting along, Jack?" she asked him.

"Fine as frog's hair," said Jack. He didn't want to let on he was having any trouble, but it was hard to ignore that big pile of manure. "Well, I guess there's not much use to lie about it," said Jack. "I ain't doing much good a-tall. I guess I'll just have to shovel faster."

"Law no, don't do that!" Molly told him. "Here, I'll help ye." Molly took the old shovel and pitched out a shovelful, and all the rest of the manure raised up in the air and went out with it. Right then they heard the giant coming back and Molly ran and hid.

"Well, did you get it cleaned out?" boomed the giant. He was one of these people that don't know any way to talk but LOUD.

"Look and see," said Jack. "Look and see."

The giant looked and saw his barn was clean as a pin. Well, you'd think he'd be pleased, but he wasn't. He flew mad as a wet hen. "Who's helped you?" he wanted to know. Jack never answered. "You've had help, I can see that. I'll catch you in it the next time," he said. Never said a word about the big sack of money. Then they all went back to the house and ate supper and went to bed.

Next day the giant had another job for Jack. "I've got some horses up here," he said, "that's not been caught in seven years. I want you to catch them horses and ride them. If you can do that today, I'll give you a big sack of money. If you can't, I'll have to cut your head off."

That part about the head still worried Jack a little, but jobs being scarce as hen's teeth around there and having no better offers, he went along with it.

The giant took Jack out to the place where the horses grazed, handed him an old bridle and a new bridle, and left him. Said he'd be back about dark. Jack took the new bridle and started trying to catch the wild horses. But every time he got close to one, it would bolt and run off up the hill. But he kept right on chasing them, Jack did, and might have been there chasing them yet if Molly hadn't come to check on him.

"Well, how you getting along, Jack?" she asked him.

"Fine as frog's hair," said Jack. But anybody could look and see that empty bridle in his hand. "Well, not the best ever was," Jack told her. "I've chased horses up one hillside and down the other till I'm give out and not caught one yet."

"Here, I'll help ye," Molly said. And she picked up the old bridle, slipped it on Raglif Jaglif Tartliff Pole, and led him into the barn lot. Then all the other horses got in line behind Raglif Jaglif and went in the barn lot, too, just like they'd been doing it all their lives. Molly and Jack rode the wild horses all evening till they heard the giant coming back, then Molly went and hid.

"Well, did you catch the horses?" boomed the giant.

"Look and see," said Jack. "Look and see."

The giant looked and saw, all right. He saw all the wild horses standing around the barn lot, very orderly and peaceful. Well, you'd think he'd be pleased, but he wasn't. "You've had help again!" he roared. "But just you wait. I'll catch you the next time." So then they all went back to the house and ate supper and went to bed and the giant never named a big sack of money that time either.

When morning came the giant was waiting. "I've got one more job for you, Jack," he said. "I need you to gather eggs for me."

Jack was glad to hear that, and he began to brag on himself, how he was the best hand to gather eggs in all creation and how fast and how big and how many and if the giant would just tell him where they was at he'd go right then and get them.

"The eggs are in a nest. The nest is in a tree. The tree is up on a rock cliff. The rock cliff is across the river," said the giant. "Nobody's gathered eggs out of that nest in seven years. If you can do it, I'll give you a big sack of money. If you can't—"

"I know," said Jack. "You don't have to say it." So Jack and the giant headed down to the riverbank where the giant kept two boats, an old boat and a new boat. Then he left Jack, said he'd be back about dark.

Jack climbed in the new boat and commenced to paddle. Paddled all morning just as hard as he could paddle and never moved one inch. But he kept on paddling pretty vigorous just the same and might have been there paddling yet if Molly Whuppie hadn't showed up. "How are you getting along, Jack?" she asked him.

Jack decided to save time and tell the truth. "I ain't doing no good a-tall," he said. "I'm paddling but I ain't getting nowhere. I'll just have to paddle faster, I reckon."

"Law no, don't do that!" Molly said. Then they got in the old boat, paddled across the river, and climbed up the rock cliff to the tree with the nest in the top. But when they got up there, they saw that tree had no limbs on it. "Can't nobody climb a tree like that," said Jack.

"I believe I can climb it," Molly said, and she took and pulled her fingers off one at a time and stuck them on the tree to make a ladder. She climbed up, got the eggs, and was about down to the ground again, sticking her fingers back on her hands as she came down, when they heard the giant coming back. Molly had to run and hide so fast, she left one finger stuck on the tree.

"Well, did you gather the eggs?" the giant wanted to know. He thought shore he'd get to cut somebody's head off that time.

"Look and see," said Jack. "Look and see."

The giant looked and saw the eggs, and he was not a bit pleased. "You've had help and I know who's helped you! I'm not paying you a penny of money, and your head comes off tonight!" He stormed off then, and Molly came out from her hidey-hole.

Well, Molly and Jack both knew they were in a dangerous situation and they had better get out of there as quick as they could. So they went and got the sacks of money the giant owed them and away they rode on Raglif Jaglif Tartliff Pole. Rode a while and they heard the giant coming up behind them, gaining fast. He was about to catch up to them, and I hate to think what would have happened next if Molly hadn't leaned over right then and sung in the horse's ear:

Raglif Jaglif Tartliff Pole
Hoof of wind and eye of coal
Carry me and my love away
Where trouble cannot follow.

Raglif Jaglif took off like the wind, buddy, and fairly flew over the ground. He took Molly and Jack so fast and so far the giant could never catch them, and he gave it up and went back to the house.

Molly and Jack rode on till they got to where Jack's people lived. Jack said he hadn't seen his mommy and his pap and his brothers Will and Tom in so long, he wanted to go stay with them a while.

"Well, we'll go," said Molly. "But you listen to me. If you let anybody else kiss you, you'll forget all about me." Well, Jack swore up and down he wouldn't.

So they went on in and Jack told them, said, "Don't kiss me." And they never. They were not much for all this hugging and kissing and carrying on, anyway, Jack's people were not. But Jack had a little old dog, and it was so pleased to see Jack after he'd been gone so long that before they could stop it, it ran and jumped and gave Jack a big buss right smack on the mouth. And sure enough, right then Jack forgot all about Molly. Didn't know who she was or a thing about her. So she had to up and leave from there and go off by herself. Fortunately she still had Raglif Jaglif with her and the money she'd made working for the giant, so she got along all right.

Well, time went along, went along, and one day Molly heard the news that Jack was about to get married to somebody else, and they were having a big dance at the schoolhouse to announce it. So Molly went to the dance, and she took three boxes with her.

A big crowd was there, and they asked her, said, "What's in them boxes?" So Molly opened one box, and out flew a hen and a rooster. The hen pecked the rooster on the neck and said, "You forgot about me cleaning out the barn that hadn't been cleaned in seven years or good-bye your head." Jack looked at Molly. Seem like he'd seen her somewhere before.

Molly opened the second box, and out flew another hen and rooster. The hen pecked the rooster on the neck and said, "You forgot about me catching the horses that hadn't been caught in seven years or good-bye your head." Jack sidled over toward Molly, and his mind began to come back to him a little.

Molly opened the third box, and out popped another hen and rooster. The hen pecked the rooster on the neck and said, "You forgot about me climbing the tree and gathering the eggs that hadn't been gathered in seven years or good-bye your head."

Then Jack looked at Molly's hand and saw where she had one finger missing, and he remembered everything. Then he went and told the other girl he was sorry but he could not marry her. If he was to marry anybody, it would have to be Molly Whuppie. Well, that girl talked pretty bad to Jack, I reckon, called him everything but a milk cow, and really, I don't blame her.

Then Jack told Molly that considering the emotion of the situation, maybe they better go on and not stay for the dancing. So they got on Raglif Jaglif and rode away, and as they rode Molly sang:

Raglif Jaglif Tartliff Pole
Hoof of wind and eye of coal
Carry me and my love away
Where trouble cannot follow.

: Molly, Jack, and the Sillies :

Molly and Jack must have got married and run through all their money pretty quick because at the start of this tale I'm fixing to tell right now, they are already married to one another and living in a little old house on the side of the hill and not doing much good at all, financially speaking.

One day Molly got to studying about a milk cow. "I wish we had us a milk cow," she said to Jack. "If we had a milk cow, we'd never have to go hungry, for we could always get milk from the cow."

Molly had some money put back—fifty dollars, I believe it was—and she went and got that money, handed it to Jack, and told him to take it to the stock sale in town and buy a good milk cow with it.

"And don't come back with a little handful of bean seeds, neither," she added. For she knew Jack had a tendency to deviate from the plan. "Just go straight to town and get the cow."

And that's exactly what Jack did. Went straight to town, picked out the prettiest cow there, paid the fifty dollars, and headed back to the house. And right then is when the trouble started.

Jack was just walking down the road, leading his new cow with a rope, when somehow or another the rope slipped out of Jack's hand. The next thing Jack knew that cow had got loose and run off up in the hill—a heap faster than you'd ever think a cow could move—and commenced a-thrashing around in the briars and bushes and got its rope all tangled up and wrapped around a sassafras tree about seventeen or eighteen times and come in a pea of choking itself to death.

Well, Jack had a time with it, but finally he got it back down on the road and headed in the right direction. But in about five minutes it got loose again and was over in the fencerow eating weeds and got tangled up in sumac and Jack like to never got it out. Finally they got started down the road one more time, walked along a few minutes, and met a woman leading a pig. The woman told Jack that shore was a pretty cow, and she asked him was it well behaved.

"Law, no," said Jack. "Hit's the worst-behaved cow in the world. Hit gets loose and runs off up in the hill and gets its rope all in a tangle and it's a chow to get it loose," said Jack.

"A cow will do that-a-way," said the woman.

Jack looked at the pig. "Does your pig do like that?" he asked her.

"Why, no," said the woman. "A pig won't do like that."

"You're lucky," said Jack. "You wouldn't want to swap with me, would you, my cow to your pig?"

The woman said why shore, she'd swap, and she took the cow and went one way, and Jack took the pig and went the other.

Jack was just thinking to himself how much better off he was to be going down the road with a pig than to be up in the briars and bushes trying to untangle a cow when he noticed the pig had got loose and was wallering around in a mud hole.

"No! Bad pig!" hollered Jack. But the pig didn't pay a bit more attention to Jack than the man in the moon. Jack was still standing there trying to talk the pig out of the mud hole when along came a man with a big brown dog.

"What seems to be the trouble?" the man asked Jack.

Well, anybody could see what the trouble was. That pig was down a-wallering in the loblolly, was all over mud from the flat of its snout to the curl of its tail, and what's more it showed no intention of ever getting up.

"Oh, it's this crazy pig," Jack complained. "Hit's got down in this mud and won't get out."

"A pig will do that," said the man.

Jack looked at the dog. "I bet that dog wouldn't get down and waller in the mud and not get out," said Jack.

"No, a dog won't do like that," said the man.

"You're lucky," said Jack. "I don't reckon you'd swap with me, would you, my pig to your dog?"

"I surely would," said the man, and he pulled the pig out of the mud and went off with it before Jack could change his mind.

Jack started on down the road with his new dog, very well pleased with himself and thinking how lucky he was to have a dog that wouldn't waller in mud or get tangled up in briars.

Well, about that time the dog spied a rabbit and took off like you'd shot it out of a cannon, and Jack after it, trying to catch up. That rabbit ran up one holler and down the next with the dog after it and Jack after the dog till finally the rabbit got away and the dog gave up and came back to where Jack was. Well, by that time Jack was completely wore out.

Got back down on the road and set down to rest a minute and along came a girl carrying a cat. "That's a pretty cat," said Jack. And it was. It was a pretty cat.

"Thank ye," said the girl. "That's a pretty dog."

"I'm mad at that dog," said Jack. "Hit's run me all over this end of the county chasing a rabbit."

"A dog will do you that-a-way," said the girl.

"Will a cat do like that?" Jack asked.

"No, a cat won't do like that," said the girl. "You can carry a cat."

"You're mighty lucky," said Jack. "I don't reckon you'd want to swap with me, would you, my dog to your cat?"

"Be glad to," said the girl, and she walked off with the big brown dog like they were the best of friends.

Jack headed on toward the house with his cat in his arms. Well, he hadn't got far when the cat decided it wanted to ride up on top of Jack's head, to get a better view, and it commenced to sink its claws down in Jack's neck and shoulders, trying to climb up there.

"Well, I can't stand this," said Jack. And he was standing there in the road trying to do something with the cat when along came a boy with a rock in his hand.

"Are you having trouble with your cat?" the boy asked Jack. Well, anybody could see that he was.

"Law, yes," said Jack. "Hit's climbed all over me, clawed me and scratched me, tore me all to pieces, and won't be still a minute."

"A cat will do you that-a-way," said the boy.

Molly, Jack, and the Sillies : : : 73

"That's a good-looking rock," said Jack. "And I bet it stays still when you carry it."

"I've not had no trouble with it," said the boy.

"You're lucky in that," said Jack. "I don't reckon you'd swap with me, would you, the cat for the rock?"

"Well, I don't know," said the boy. He'd have to think on it a minute. It was an awful good rock. He was aiming to take it home to his mommy for a doorstop, and a cat would not be the same thing. He reckoned he better keep it.

But Jack looked so disappointed that the boy gave in and said, all right, he'd trade. And he pulled the cat off of Jack's head and handed Jack the rock.

Finally Jack made it back home with his rock, but Molly was not so well pleased with it as he hoped she'd be. "Where's my cow?" she asked him, the minute he walked in the door.

"I swapped it to a pig," said Jack.

"Where's the pig?"

"Swapped it to a dog."

"Where's the dog?"

"Swapped it to a cat."

"Where's the cat?"

"The cat is what I had to trade to get this rock," Jack explained, as if that ought to clear the matter up once and for all.

"Well, that beats all I ever heard," said Molly. And she let Jack know in no uncertain terms that she was not a bit impressed with his trading abilities and, in fact, was convinced he must be the foolishest man in the world.

"Oh, no," Jack replied modestly. "They's plenty of men as foolish as me."

"I very much doubt it," said Molly, and she went and put her hat on, which Jack thought was not a good sign.

Molly said she was so mad at Jack she couldn't stand to look at him and was leaving him and not to expect her home till she had found three men as foolish as Jack and got her fifty dollars back, too.

Before Jack could think of a word to say, Molly had slammed the door, stomped off the porch, and was around the curve and gone, leaving Jack alone with his rock.

Molly walked all that evening. She figured she would have to walk a long way to find three men as foolish as Jack and get her fifty dollars back, too.

The sun went down and the moon came up, a big round yellow moon that almost made the night as bright as the day, and Molly kept walking. Directly she heard somebody a-hollering over in a field beside the road, sounded like something was bad wrong. So naturally she ran right over there to see if she could help some way. But when she got over there all she found was a man a-standing by the edge of a pond, staring at the moon's reflection on the water.

"You scared me to death," said Molly. "I thought shore something was bad the matter."

"Hit is!" that feller hollered. "Cain't you see? The moon has done fell in the pond! We've got to git it out!"

Well, Molly saw right then he was crazy as a bedbug. She tried to get him to calm down and listen to reason, but of course he would not, just kept hollering the moon was in the pond and begging her to go tell his brother to come with the mule and pull it out. Said he'd give her ten dollars if she would.

So Molly did what he asked her to, put the ten dollars in her apron pocket, and went on down the road. "Well, that's one," she said.

The next day Molly was going along the road, looked over and saw a man and a woman plowing. There wouldn't have been anything unusual in that if the man hadn't a-been using the woman for a plowhorse. And to beat it all there stood a big good horse under a shade tree munching grass.

"What in the world are you a-doing?" Molly asked that man. "Why are you using this poor woman for a plow-horse when you've got a good horse right here?"

"Well, since you asked me I'll tell you," he said. "I don't know how to hook the horse to the plow lines."

"Well, if that's all that's the matter," Molly told him, "I can show you how to put the plow lines on in five minutes."

The woman turned around then. "Honey, if you could do that," she said, "it would be worth a big lot to me. You show him how to hook the plow lines to the horse, and I'll pay you twenty dollars."

Molly showed the man what all to do, and he started plowing with the horse. The woman handed Molly a twenty-dollar bill, then headed for the porch to sit in a rocker, put her feet up on the railing, and light her pipe. Molly tucked that twenty-dollar bill in her apron pocket and went on down the road. "Well, that's two," she said.

Walked on down the road and was going by some houses when she heard somebody hollering their head off, sounded like somebody trying to kill somebody. Looked over there and saw a man and a woman out on the front porch. The man was sitting in a chair and he had something over his head, and the woman was standing right behind him a-beating him over the head with a boat paddle. And he was hollering bloody murder.

"What in the world do you think you're a-doing?" Molly asked that woman, said, "You're about to beat this poor man to death."

"I know it," said the woman, and you could tell she felt bad about it. "But I don't know no other way to get his head through the neck of his shirt," she said. "Ever year I make him a new shirt. I can fix the front and the back and the sleeves and the buttons, but I don't know how to make a neck hole. So we have to do it like this. It's hard on him, I know, bless his heart." The man whimpered under his new shirt. "Just one more good lick or two ort to do it," she told him. And she rared back to whomp him with the boat paddle again.

"Hold it a minute," said Molly, and she grabbed the paddle out of the woman's hand. "I can show you how to make the neck hole of a shirt."

Well, that man was so happy to hear them words he began to sob. "Law, honey, if you could do that," he said, "I'd be so grateful I'd pay ye twenty dollars."

Molly showed the woman how to fix the neck hole of a shirt, took the twenty dollars, and left them both a-standing there waving good-bye.

"Well, that's three," Molly said. And she turned around and started back the other way, toward Jack and home.

Jack was tickled to death to see her. And he told her, now that he'd had time to think on it, he could see where she was right about the cow and the pig and the dog and the cat and the rock and all.

Molly said Jack was right about something, too. There was a heap of silly men in the world. And some silly women, too.

: Just Past Dreaming Rock :

Days passed and nights passed. Weeks passed and months passed. Years rolled by, and even Molly Whuppie got old. And when she was old she lived by herself, up on Big Lonesome, just the other side of Dreaming Rock, in a house painted yellow with a creek running alongside and a big burr oak in the yard.

And she was well satisfied. Got so she stayed at the house a big lot of the time. Now Molly Whuppie was lively even in old age, but she just couldn't go out and fight giants every day of the week like she used to. Besides, the times were a-changing. Young people were coming up and taking over the giant-fighting business, and they had new technologies and philosophies and methodologies, and it was only right and proper that they did. But that meant business was down and not much money coming in.

But if Molly Whuppie had two biscuits to her name, she would give one to you. Or to anybody else that happened by and needed a biscuit. If they needed a bed to sleep in, a place to stay a while, a little money to tide them over, or just somebody to listen to their troubles and not try to boss, it didn't matter who it was, Molly Whuppie would take them in and welcome, she was that good-hearted. For she remembered many a night when she was a stranger out on the road, with no supper in her belly and nowhere to lay her head, and how good it was to meet a body with a kind heart and a gentle way about them.

So the house painted yellow with the creek alongside and the big burr oak in the yard never did go long without company. And every stray dog or cat that trotted down the pike, no matter how scruffy, scraggly, mean, mangy, and generally unpromising it appeared to be, Molly Whuppie would take it in, feed it, doctor it, and pet it. So naturally none of them would ever leave, and it got to where she had about thirty or forty dogs around the place and too many cats to count.

One night Molly Whuppie went to sleep and she dreamed a dream. She dreamt she saw a mule pulling a wagon with the rainbow in it, and the mule called her by her name. "Molly Whuppie," it said, "go to town and perk up your ears."

Molly didn't remember the dream when she first woke up the next morning, but it came back to her all of a sudden and she had to sit down a minute and think. It might mean something. Or it might not. It was hard to tell about dreams.

Well, there was just one way to find out. Molly Whuppie tied her bonnet around her neck and headed straight to the town square, where she sat on a bench under a shade tree all day long and kept her ears open. But all she heard was the usual gossip—crops, hunting dogs, the weather, predestination—nothing unusual in that. Molly went home and tried to put the whole business out of her mind.

But mules pulled rainbows through her dreams again that night, saying, "Go to town, Molly Whuppie, and perk up your ears." So when day broke Molly went and sat on a bench in the town square all that day with her ears perked up again, but she didn't hear anything that day neither, nothing she hadn't heard a thousand times before. Molly got home tired that night and decided that would be the last time she planned her schedule around advice from a talking mule.

But that night she dreamed the same dream again. And everybody knows if you dream the same thing three nights running, you better pay attention. So this time, Molly didn't even go back to sleep, just laid there waiting for daylight to come, so she could get to town and be there and ready for whatever it was that was going to happen.

Well, she sat there all day again, and not one thing happened that was worth telling about. Toward dark Molly Whuppie got up and started home.

Just at the edge of town she heard somebody coming up behind her. Turned around and there was a young man standing there. "I know it ain't none of my business," he said, "but I was wanting to ask you something."

"Spit it out," said Molly Whuppie.

The feller said he worked at the bank in the square, and for the past three days every time he looked out the window he saw Molly Whuppie sitting on that bench. And he was just curious as to why.

Molly told him about the mule and the rainbow and all, and he laughed. "Now that's the difference between you and me," he said. "I dream foolishness like that all the time, and I don't pay a bit of attention to it. Last night I dreamed I heard a cow up in the pulpit preaching, and it told me to go out in the country to a house painted yellow with a creek running alongside and to dig under a big burr oak till I found a box full of silver and gold." He stopped to chuckle at the foolishness of it. "Now if I paid attention to dreams," he went on, "I'd be running all over the countryside digging holes in the ground and they would lock me up for a loony."

Molly Whuppie didn't hear that last part about the loony. She took off right after the part about the box full of silver and gold and was back home in no time and out under the big burr oak with a shovel and a lantern.

She dug and struck tree roots. She dug and struck rocks. She dug and struck broken pie plates and rusty bucket lids. But she found no gold and silver. Then her shovel struck something else.

The old wooden box had decayed from staying so long in the damp ground, but the silver and gold, when the lantern light hit it, still shone bright as the day that somebody, now long gone, had buried it in the ground.

Molly silently thanked them, whoever they were and wherever they were, and thanked the mule with the rainbow, too.

Next day she took some of the gold and silver to town and put it in the bank. The young feller that worked there teased her about the dream again, but Molly didn't care what he said.

That money has lasted Molly Whuppie to this day. And the fun she has had a-spending it, and the good she has done a-sharing it, well, you never saw the beat of it in your life.

So if you ever find yourself out on the road, up Big Lonesome just past Dreaming Rock, and you need a place to stay, a bite to eat, or just somebody to talk to, keep on the lookout for a house painted yellow with a creek running alongside and a big burr oak in the yard. March right up and knock on the door. You'll be welcome, I guarantee.

In the meantime, remember your dreams. Memorize a few magic words in case of an emergency. Be kind to the ones you meet on the road. And you might want to carry a little flat rock in your pocket.

: About the Stories :

I was visiting Goose Rock Elementary School in Clay County, Kentucky, trying with limited success to drag a roomful of sleepy fifth graders through a series of writing exercises. I sneaked a look at my watch. Twenty minutes to go. "Wanna hear a story?" I asked.

I knew only two then, well enough to tell them, "Jack in the Giant's Newground" and "Jack and the Doctor's Girl," both from Richard Chase's collection of Jack tales. I can't remember which one I told, but when I walked into class the next day, I was amazed to find these same kids up on their feet acting out "Jack and the Northwest Wind." Without being told to, they had gone to the school library, checked out *The Jack Tales*, and started reading the stories and acting out the parts. I knew we were onto something.

What we were onto, of course, was what people all over the world have been onto for a very long time now: the power and magic of the folktale. I began studying folktales in earnest, going to storytelling festivals, telling stories myself whenever and wherever anybody would let me. I was familiar with the work of Leonard Roberts—a folklorist, folklore professor, writer, and native of Eastern Kentucky—from Gerald Alvey's folklore class at the University of Kentucky. I began rereading Roberts's delightful collections of folktales from Eastern Kentucky: *I Bought Me a Dog, Nippy and the Yankee Doodle, Old Greasybeard, South from Hell-fer-Sartin,* and *Up Cutshin and Down Greasy.* I have employed other sources here, but I have relied most on Roberts's fieldwork for the stories in this collection.

I loved the language in Roberts's tales, those surprising turns of phrase, so old they sound fresh again, that characterize traditional Appalachian speech. In a way, reading the tales was like going home.

Growing up in Eastern Kentucky in the 1950s, I had not heard stories like these. A strong oral tradition persisted in family stories, personal stories, ghost stories, and local legends, but in the communities I knew as a child, the old European fairy tales had been largely forgotten. I had not heard stories like these, but I had heard talk like this at the country store my grandparents kept, around my father's family's homeplace, and at home. My parents, both teachers, knew the conventions of standard English, but their speech was liberally and lovingly flavored with the expressions they had grown up with in southeastern Kentucky.

The tales Leonard Roberts collected were rich in that traditional Appalachian way of talking, and one of the goals of this collection has been to celebrate and preserve that. As a folklorist, Roberts did his job well, setting down the tales just as they came to him. But my job was different. As a writer and storyteller I have felt free, as storytellers always have, to adapt the tales to my own time and tastes. Telling them in schools, libraries, and festivals, I was gratified to see how well these tales still captivated listeners. But some things had to change.

The old tales carry with them our inherited cultural values, our beliefs in courage, compassion, and the supernatural. Some carry other cultural values, too—racism, sexism, ageism, and other prejudices. It was easy enough to reject the tales that denigrate African Americans or the Irish, but the stories' traditional view of women could not be gotten around so easily. It was built into the plots, in which the hero, usually a man or boy, embarks on a journey, encounters adversaries of various types, and thereby displays his cleverness, his courage, and his connection to the spiritual. Female characters tend to play much more passive roles. The tales' gender stereotyping seemed anachronistic, and it was not something I was interested in passing on.

I began to look for stories with a woman or girl as their main character, and I found them. They exist in the oral traditions of cultures all over the world, though they represent only a small fraction of the total body of folktales. In British tradition, I found a character named Molly Whuppie who shared many attributes with Jack, of beanstalk fame. She encountered some of the same foes and dispatched them with the same combination of nerve, trickery, magic, and luck. And she had a great name. I decided to assign to Molly Whuppie some of the adventures I had found assigned to other heroes, both female and male. In choosing the stories, I had only two criteria: I had to have some evidence of the story's having been told in the Appalachian region, and I had to like it.

Although I have not provided full annotations for the stories, I have made an honest attempt, in the following paragraphs and in the list of sources, to identify major sources and to shed some light on the process by which the stories came to their present form. My methods in developing the stories have been those of the poet and storyteller rather than the scholar and folklorist. I have spent a great deal of time in the 398.2 sections of school and public libraries; I have heard many good storytellers, professional and otherwise; and I have been privileged to live in Eastern Kentucky most of my life, soaking up examples of colorful expressions and humorous understatement. I have told, written, and rewritten these tales dozens of times over a number of years, telling them a little differently each time, pulling things, as I needed them, like Molly pulling rocks from her pocket, from reading, personal experience, memory, and imagination. I offer the following comments on some of the stories, in the order in which they appear in the text, as examples of my sources and how I have employed them.

"The Adventures of Molly Whuppie" is my adaptation of the only story I have found in print or oral tradition using the name "Molly Whuppie." It appeared in Joseph Jacobs's *English Fairy Tales* in 1890 and has been included in numerous collections since, usually titled simply "Molly Whuppie." My version is closest to the story "Merrywise" found in two of Leonard Roberts's collections: *I Bought Me a Dog* and *South from Hell-fer-Sartin*.

Roberts offers another version in *Up Cutshin and Down Greasy*: "Polly, Nancy, and Munciemeg." Since this is clearly the old Molly Whuppie story, it connects the British Molly Whuppie to the Appalachian girl hero

Munciemeg, found in Roberts's tales collected in Eastern Kentucky, and to Mutsmag, whom Richard Chase found in western North Carolina. Molly Whuppie, like the better-known Jack, had crossed the Atlantic to America and found a home in the mountains. But her name, like the names of other immigrants, had changed a bit in the process. I liked the old name better.

This tale usually begins with the three girls getting left "in a wood" by their parents, who are too poor to feed them. I preferred to begin rather more cheerfully, with the sisters going on a journey. I changed the woman character from a witch to a giant, reasoning that women in stories should get to be giants sometimes, as well as giant fighters, and that we probably have enough witches in stories already.

Like Roberts's "Merrywise," and unlike most other versions, mine drops the stealing-from-a-giant episodes and substitutes the throwing back of magic articles as obstacles for the pursuer. I also picked up from Roberts's "Merrywise" the motifs of the "puddin-tuddin bag" and the "seven-mile-step boots." I named Molly's two sisters—unnamed in the British version—Poll and Betts, after Mutsmag's sisters in Chase's *Grandfather Tales*.

I have two sources for the exact wording I attribute to the helpful bird in the story: the title story from Roberts's *Nippy and the Yankee Doodle*; and a man I once knew here on Teges Creek who would suddenly exclaim, quite loudly and for no apparent reason, "Daub it with moss and stick it with clay!"

I based the story "Molly the Giant Slayer" on "Jack Outwits the Giants" in Roberts's *I Bought Me a Dog* and *South from Hell-fer-Sartin*, the only sources I have for it. In this story, as in others, I have altered or deleted incidents in which people seem to be unnecessarily beating one another to bloody pulps with clubs and things. Here, however, I retained the two giant decapitations on the grounds of their being essential to the plot.

There are countless versions of the good-sister/bad-sister story. Mine, "Molly and Blunderbore," is closest to "The Two Gals" in Roberts's *Up*

Cutshin and Down Greasy. It is also kin to "Gallymanders Gallymanders" in Chase's *Grandfather Tales*, both of them being descended from the Grimms' "Mother Holle." In Chase and Grimm, the sisters are pursued by a stingy old woman, whom I changed into a boring old giant, borrowing the name Blunderbore from the giant Jack took on in "Jack the Giant Killer" from Roberts's *Nippy and the Yankee Doodle*.

"Molly Fiddler" is based on "Freddy and His Fiddle" in Roberts's *Old Greasybeard*.

"Runaway Cornbread" (or, "The Little Red Hen Meets the Fleeing Pancake") comes from "The Three Mice" in Roberts's *Old Greasybeard*. I enlarged the beginning, changed the ending, and, desirous to save the cornbread's life, provided a hole for it to jump down, like the old woman's dumpling in the folktale from Japan.

In "Molly and the Ogre Who Would Not Pick Up," I began with Roberts's "The Little Blue Ball" in *South from Hell-fer-Sartin*, then added the poet and the fight with the ogre. Molly got the idea to "job" the ogre's foot with a needle from Little One Inch, the Japanese folktale hero who defeats the monster by jumping into its mouth and poking its tongue with a needle, which Little One Inch carries for a sword.

Both Leonard Roberts (in *Up Cutshin and Down Greasy*) and Marie Campbell (in *Tales from the Cloud Walking Country*) report having collected versions of "The Old Woman and Her Pig" in Eastern Kentucky, though Roberts does not include the story in his print collections, and Campbell's version is very like other print forms. I had a lot of fun with "Pig Tale," elaborating on the beginning and giving the old woman a boyfriend at the end. In the middle, I changed the more grisly parts so the reader, to get to the happy ending, does not have to step over the bodies of a hanged butcher and a slaughtered ox.

"Jack and the Christmas Beans" is my own invention, using some familiar motifs.

"Molly and Jack" is based on "Raglif Jaglif Tartliff Pole" in Roberts's *I Bought Me a Dog* and *Old Greasybeard*.

Clearly I am most indebted to Leonard Roberts, whose work inspired half the stories in this collection and contributed to the spirit of all of them. Roberts's books and other works are included in the list of sources. But I am indebted to others as well.

I have enjoyed and learned from many storytellers, including Angelyn DeBord, Elizabeth Ellis, Mary Hamilton, Orville Hicks, Ray Hicks, Randy Wilson, and another wonderful storyteller, my father-in-law, Robert Shelby, of Corbin, Kentucky.

I thank my agent Deborah Carter of Muse Literary Management, and I thank the Kentucky Foundation for Women, which supported, in part, the research and writing of the book.

I want to thank, too, those friends, colleagues, and kinfolks who have been with me in valuing and remembering our traditional Appalachian ways of talking and telling, especially Silas House, Jason Howard, Jamie Johnson, Gurney Norman, Marianne Worthington, and most of all, the good sister, Jessie Lynne Gabbard Keltner.

Now I am about to say the thing storytellers always say when they publish print collections. These stories are meant to be told. I hope they will please adults and older children who read them on their own. I hope that parents, teachers, librarians, and others will read them aloud to younger children. And I hope that readers and listeners of all ages will make these stories their own, and keep them alive, by telling and retelling them in their own ways.

Anne Shelby
Teges, Kentucky
January 2007

SOURCES

Campbell, Marie. *Tales from the Cloud Walking Country*. Bloomington: Indiana University Press, 1958.

Chase, Richard. *Grandfather Tales*. Boston: Houghton Mifflin, 1948.

———. *Jack and the Three Sillies*. Boston: Houghton Mifflin, 1950.

———. *The Jack Tales*. Boston: Houghton Mifflin, 1943.

Cole, Joanna. *Best Loved Folktales of the World*. New York: Doubleday, 1982.

Minard, Rosemary. *Womenfolk and Fairy Tales*. Boston: Houghton Mifflin, 1975.

Roberts, Leonard W. *I Bought Me a Dog and Other Folktales from the Southern Mountains*. Berea, Ky.: Council of the Southern Mountains, 1954.

———. *Nippy and the Yankee Doodle and More Folk Tales from the Southern Mountains*. Berea, Ky.: Council of the Southern Mountains, 1958.

———. *Old Greasybeard: Tales from the Cumberland Gap*. Detroit: Folklore Associates, 1969.

———. *South from Hell-fer-Sartin: Kentucky Mountain Folk Tales*. Lexington: University Press of Kentucky, 1955.

———. *Up Cutshin and Down Greasy: Folkways of a Kentucky Mountain Family*. Lexington: University Press of Kentucky, 1959.

Sakade, Florence. *Japanese Children's Favorite Stories*. Rutland, Vt.: Charles E. Tuttle, 1958.